To Jack with
fond memories,
Paul

CODE RED

CODE RED

PAUL A. REYFF

This book is a work of historical fiction.

"Code Red," by Paul A. Reyff. ISBN 978-1-60264-524-0.

Published 2010 by Virtualbookworm.com Publishing Inc., P.O. Box 9949, College Station, TX 77842, US.

Manufactured in the United States of America.

Dedication

To my 5 year-old grandson, Jon Paul, born into a
dangerous world:
You will be inspired by the courage of our forebears
and make this a safer world for all.

AUTHOR'S NOTE

All the major events and their dates recounted in this story are matters of historical record. It is their interpretation that has been missing, now for almost seventy years. Because of that passage of time, I have used the actual names of most of the participants, and their diaries or recollections, without fear of violating anyone's privacy.

The focal point of this story — the race for the development of atomic weapons and the failure of an evil regime to achieve that goal — is as much a priority in international affairs now as it was, in its infancy, then. Then, it was in the context of World War II, and a desperate gamble to keep the atomic bomb away from Nazi Germany, even as that country was pushing the limits of warfare, from jet aircraft to warheads delivered by rockets.

I am indebted to many public and private records in putting all the pieces of this puzzle together. The heroes of the story have all been appropriately recognized elsewhere; my purpose here is only to show how they fit into a larger canvas, even though none of them, I suspect, knew it at the time.

The villains of this story are the usual ones, and they are still with us: fear and defeatism in the face of evil. One young man, early in that great war, showed how courage can overcome those villains. This is his story.

TABLE OF CONTENTS

TWENTY-EIGHT: June 21, 1942, Berchtesgaden, Germany
TWENTY-NINE: June 21, 1942 Bora Bora, Fiji Islands
THIRTY: July 20, 1942 Berkeley, California
THIRTY-ONE: August 12, 1942, Melbourne, Australia
THIRTY-TWO: August 20, 1942, Stockholm, Sweden
THIRTY-THREE: September 1, 1942, Durban, South Africa
THIRTY-FOUR: September 15, 1942, Richmond, California
THIRTY-FIVE: September 22, 1942, Libreville, French
    Equatorial Africa
THIRTY-SIX: September 23, 1942, Capetown, South Africa
THIRTY-SEVEN: September 27, 1942, South Atlantic
THIRTY-EIGHT: September 29, 1942, Reich Chancellery,
    Berlin
THIRTY-NINE: October 2, 1942, Richmond, California
FORTY: October 20, 1942, Recife, Brazil

I have raised a monument more lasting than bronze....

Horace

PROLOGUE

It is a day ten years ago. It is today. It is a day ten years from now. Mid-afternoon summer heat on the east coast produces oppressive conditions for any type of heavy physical activity outdoors. For the Plebes marching in the hot sun on Barney Square, it could hardly get worse. For the past hour, sweat had poured off their freshly shaved heads while drill instructors shouted orders at the top of their lungs. "Indoctrination" was well underway at the United States Merchant Marine Academy in Kings Point, New York.

Young men and women, most fresh out of high school, are quickly learning how to survive this three month ordeal to better prepare themselves for the rigors ahead of them. It is an old military tradition. Tear the student down so that they can be re-built in the military way so they have the best possible chance in their future careers as officers in what is commonly referred to as the fourth arm of defense and a dwindling American industry. Only half of the men and women marching that hot August afternoon would survive the rigors and graduate from the Academy.

Across the well trimmed grounds of the campus, another group of Plebes is about to learn how to command the Monomoy. Each Plebe would test their command acumen, maneuvering judgment and physical stamina in these two thousand pound rowboats which were direct descendents from the whalers used off Cape Cod nearly three centuries ago. A Plebe, late for the Monomoy instruction on the waterfront, was running by a statue of a young man dressed in the simple mariner's clothing of a time gone by. The Plebe, who could well have been a model for this massive bronze figure, took notice of this lonely figure standing an eternal watch over the waters of Long Island Sound.

Not entirely focused on where he was going, the Plebe nearly runs into an upperclassman, dressed in his summer khakis, descending the steps behind the statue. The upperclassman, sensing an opportunity to carry on a ritual so steeped in maritime tradition, demands to know the Plebe's last name and the regimental company he has been assigned to. Clearly startled and practically shaking, the young man pulls himself upright and provides satisfactory answers. The upperclassman then asks "How many merchant mariners were killed in World War II?"

"One hundred forty two, SIR!"

Not satisfied to let this Plebe off easily, the upperclassman shouts "Who was the first midshipman to be killed in World War II?"

"I, ah—"

"Name him!"

"I think it was... Edwin O'Hara, SIR."

"You don't think mister!" You either know, or you don't know. IS THAT CLEAR !

Yes, SIR.

"Now, who was the first midshipman killed in World War II?"

"Edwin O'Hara, SIR."

"Carry-on mister. You are late for class."

The Plebe was gone.

The upperclassman, pleased with his own performance as much as that of the Plebes, set his sights on the next pack of krill heading his way on the training grounds of this little known, but perhaps most respected maritime institution in the world. In the academies of the military services, such 'hazing' has a long tradition and is an essential element in the parsing and training of the talent pool for these future officers. The U.S. merchant marine retains a special place in

American history that all Americans would do well to remember. Its shining moment was indeed the Second World War. The merchant marine was the lifeline of armaments and supplies to all branches of the U.S. armed forces, serving in every ocean of the world.

The upper classmen at the Academy who challenge the Plebes to know the history of their institution are quite serious. After four years of service at the Academy and across the world's oceans, they understand that traditions of service count not only to their industry, but also to their country. Every midshipman is expected to live by a tradition taught at the Academy that quite literally means "Deeds, not words."

The handsome 19-year-old Californian depicted in the statue lived by these words. Edwin J. O'Hara was on his first tour of duty aboard a Liberty ship that was itself on a maiden voyage around the world. This young man was thrust into a battle that was the only encounter of surface vessels of Germany and the United States in the entire course of the war. He became the first casualty from the United States Merchant Marine Academy in World War II.

This is a story of simple convictions and bravery that quite literally changed the course of the war. This story has never before been told.
Acta, non verba.

ONE

November 11, 1992. Land's End, San Francisco

The last lingering lines of the Navy Hymn hung in the air for a respectful minute before Frank Jordan, Mayor of San Francisco, broke the silence by striding to the remnants of the bridge of USS San Francisco to unveil a plaque. It was the fiftieth anniversary of the naval battle of Guadalcanal. A group of five survivors of the battle raised their eyes from the dress-white Navy band and, uncharacteristically for men who prided themselves on toughness in public, joined hands. Judson Callaghan, son of the admiral blown off the bridge in the first salvos of the battle, stood clear-eyed in the center; he had seen the action from his PT-boat as he and his crew crashed into the blackness of that night. Bob Gibson, red-cheeked six-footer, had plunged his Douglas Dauntless dive bomber into the melee several times. The three others were engine men who had actually survived the fiery scuttling of the cruiser, Daniel Judson Callaghan's flagship.

The Noon sun was rapidly clearing fog from Ocean Beach below to the Golden Gate above: the bridge was now burnt-orange, shielded in a cloud though the bay below was awash in sunlight. Though it was Veteran's Day, only a few cars had found this lonely outpost of patriotism. Children climbed on Callaghan's steel-gray bridge, stopping only to watch the mayor complete the serious-looking ceremony.

And completed it was: by a blast of trumpets from the band, the victory call of warriors of every stripe, from the plains of Marathon to the steppes of Russia. It was done with flair. In a few minutes the cars were brought around, watches were checked. It was a fine moment, it was enough. Now it was time to re-assemble somewhere else in the City for refreshments and stories about the heroics of the past.

An old woman made her way from the picnic tables at the end of the parking lot to the now-empty viewing area in front of the relic, the heavy cruiser's bridge. She rested on her cane for a few minutes, trying to make out the wording on the plaque. Everyone was soon gone, the families with their children, even the seagulls, it seemed. The shimmering crescent of the Pacific ocean stunned her with its eternal silence. But suddenly her reverie was broken.

"Did you know someone on this ship?"

The woman thought for a moment, then turned to answer. "No."

"Forgive me, but you must have had a strong reason for coming today. Your cab driver…"

"I always go somewhere on Veteran's Day."

"You had a husband in the service…"

"A son. It's been fifty years."

"I'm George Townsend," he said. "I'm of your son's generation. May I tell you why I'm here?"

"Please, I must be going. You can walk me to the cab."

As he walked, he found what he was looking for — a small gold insignia on the lapel of her jacket. He knew the next question to ask.

"You may not know this, but I've been looking for you. Your son wasn't in the Navy, was he?"

"No. The merchant marine."

"He was on the *Hopkins*, wasn't he?"

"How could you know that?"

"I was there."

TWO

November 11, 1938, Hilversum, The Netherlands,

"You contend you are here for a chess tournament," the white-haired clerk said with raised eyebrows. "It was not my understanding that women played chess, or at least, not very well."

"My son is playing. It's an international tournament. I believe Alekhine is playing…"

"Well-well! So we have an expert here…." His eyes searched over the small, fifty-ish looking woman sitting plaintively before him. Not bad, he thought — but too bony for me. Too motherly. She'd bore me after a week, even with that angelic face. But the diamond ring on her left hand — there must be something more behind that! "It's just my job, you understand, but I don't believe you. First, Herr Alekhine is nowhere near here — he's in Buenos Aires, on an exhibition tour. You know about exhibition tours? And after that, he's going to captain the German team at the Olympiad. Do you believe in the written word?" The portly, red-faced man quietly opened a desk drawer, produced a dog-eared magazine, and carefully placed it in front of her.

She ignored it. "I am Elisa Meitner, and all I want is to enter Holland. Is that asking too much?"

"What about your son? The chessplayer? Well?"

"I don't have a son. I just thought a simple reason would —"

" —would bamboozle me? Madame Meitner, this is the German Embassy, not a British pub. And I warn you — we don't take bribes. Not even… diamond rings…. I'm afraid I'll have to let the Gestapo make the decision." The clerk let out a groan as he rose from his chair, as if to signal the weight of his work and the finality of his decision. "You understand, don't you? A passport is one thing. But people don't just come and go in and out of Germany these days, on a whim. These are dangerous times…."

The woman stared ahead blankly. Is this where it's going to end, even before it's begun? Then she stood up also, opened her purse, and spilled its contents on the desk. "Do you see this? This is what I have to show for working in Germany all my life. I don't want any sympathy. I just want to leave, quietly. Can't you see this?"

"Juden?"

"Of course."

"You people should have left long ago. But I have my orders. If you tell the truth, even the Gestapo might consider you better somewhere else than *here*. Come!"

The two figures, one as thin as an actress and the other as beefy as a wrestler, joined a line in an outer office — some standing, some sprawled on the floor. When their time came, the wrestler and the actress entered a flag-draped room, the swastika and photo of Hitler hung on either side of broad windows, and stood before a long double-desk, clean except for two neatly arranged stacks of papers. Behind the desk was an athletic young man, hatless, who could have passed for an advertising executive except for the all-enveloping signs of the military, from a uniform replete with medallions to a dueling scar across his left cheek.

"Ah, what have we here?" he started cheerily, staring fiercely into the woman's eyes. At that instant she knew from long experience with junior bureaucrats that she would win this first skirmish. He would try to outwit her, but she had played that game many times before — as an attractive woman in a male-obsessed society.

The clerk began to explain: "Miss Meitner was not altogether honest with me, and so I—"

"I'm proud to say I'm a scientist, Herr Capitan," she interrupted. " But look what science has got me."

"Your papers, please."

She once again disgorged the contents of her purse, and fished out her credentials from the university. "My actual name is Lise, even though they're still using my Austrian name on all the documents. You know how the academics are…"

"The bureaucracy."

"I imagine it's true even in your — organization."

"Hmmm. Well I see the Kaiser Wilhelm Institute is losing one of its most promising physicists…"

"Promising?"

"We read the papers, don't we, Herman? By the way, you may go now. And in the future please treat women of this caliber with more respect."

"But I—"

"You may go now." As the door closed behind the befuddled clerk, the officer behind the desk swiveled in his chair and spoke to the open window behind him. "You may think the new Germany is, perhaps, aggressive, but look how far we have come in just five years. As a physicist, you see that around you, every day. You have the money to support your research. The best scientists have been coming here from all over Europe — and even from America. To Berlin. To Goetingen. Isn't this true?"

"It seems to me they're now *leaving*."

The Captain swiveled around furiously to meet her eyes. She knew what he was thinking: what you, a woman, argue with my facts? He tapped his pencil on the desk. "Herr Hahn isn't leaving, is he? You work with him—"

"I apologize—"

"No need for an apology. Perhaps I should apologize for the Anschluss — after all, it was your country that rejoined us."

"Austria will always be… Austria. I was born in Vienna, and let me tell you, Berlin was not Vienna."

"But what city gave you your science? What city gave you more than waltzes and pastries?" He opened a drawer and tore a sheet from a pad. After scribbling for a few seconds he stamped the sheet with a seal. "You win. But wherever you go, remember that there is some advantage to being well known, for your science, to an officer of the German Reich. I will send a letter to Otto Hahn and inform him that his vouching for you was respected. Now get the hell out of here!"

Lise Meitner paced back and forth on a half-flooded street of Hilversum, a quaint Dutch medieval farming town, and studied a train schedule. First to Amsterdam, there to arrange some contacts she had memorized from her Berlin colleagues. She went over their names, familiar only from papers she had read in the journals: Brock, Eulenbergh. Then the ferry to Copenhagen, and perhaps a meeting with someone at the Niels Bohr Institute. Maybe, just maybe, with her first test of the Gestapo behind her, she could actually make a life abroad, after all her years living as a German.

The Dutch train to Amsterdam was filled, ominously, with refugees from across the continent, their threadbare lives laid out in public in their over-stuffed canvas bags and coarse clothes. Yet the cacophony of Slavic voices and their scrapping children gave her an unexpected feeling of home, of the homeliness of her Austrian village of her birth. She unconsciously adjusted her 'wedding ring' as she watched the placid Dutch farmland roll by. From the first time she had come to Berlin, almost three decades ago, with a letter of recommendation to Max Planck tucked in her handbag, she was now adrift. She had witnessed the Great War as a conscripted nurse, and the sight and smell of broken bodies coming back from the front had drummed into her the emptiness of heroic slogans. She had survived the chaos after the war, the hunger and the humiliation. And now she was seeing even worse — the demonizing of 'those at fault,' those of different races or classes blamed for the failures of statesmanship.

If that wedding ring had ever been possible for her, with any of the rugged young men who shared her laboratory, it had all been lost in the upheavals of this ill-starred century. So she caressed the ring again as the outskirts of Amsterdam came into view. Perhaps, even at her age, she mused... but no. The important arc of her life's work was just ahead of her, just in reach of the right laboratory.

As the train platform in the heart of Amsterdam emptied, Meitner lingered in the hope of someone approaching with some kind of recognition. Hahn had promised all the contacts at his disposal. What a buddy, she thought — if only he hadn't already been married when she arrived in Berlin. Ah, but they often talked about how the little *frisson* between a man and a woman, not married to each other, but married to an idea, can be a delicate spice. This was gone forever, and now, what?

Meitner walked to the great concourse of buses and trains in front of the station, and waited. But for what? There were a thousand ways signals could have been lost. How safe was Hahn, himself, for having given her letters of introduction? She decided to walk to one of the famous canals of the city, where at least she could collect herself. It was peaceful, and safe, still not yet dusk. Two men who approached her along the canal appeared lost in their evening papers. Then: "Frau Meitner, unless you are a vision!"

"I'm a mess."

"We thought you'd be so much older..."

"Already I'm in love with the Dutch! Where the hell have you been?!"

"Believe it or not, nothing is safe around here. We've been following you, just to make sure all three of us don't get nabbed at the same time." The three hugged each other — two strapping young men and a frail-looking, gray-haired sprite. They split up, the younger man running ahead to find space on the late ferry to Copenhagen. It would be close. Meitner and her new-found friend, known before now only in correspondence, walked briskly but in intense conversation toward the wharves. Only Hahn was allowed to attend international conferences from the Institute. This was her first personal contact with another physicist. But they avoided all talk of the laboratory.

"The war has already begun," her young friend said. "Did the Austrians have a choice?"

"Did the Jews in Berlin have a choice? I was so naïve..."

"So don't wait for the declaration. That's a formality. Hitler will take us, because he needs the Atlantic, top to bottom. Denmark — not worth the effort. Up north, forget it. So you'll have some space in either Copenhagen or Stockholm."

The two Dutch physicists stood along side Meitner as she presented her papers at the boarding dock. The ferry was crowded, ready to sail, past the timetable for departure. "Is there any reason you couldn't wait until the morning?" the agent offered. "It's a much more scenic trip during the day, and not so crowded…."

"I'm late for a conference," she insisted, fingering the diamond ring. Was this the time to offer it, as Hahn had advised? "It's your last shot. Save it for the end," he had said, as he gave her his mother's prized possession.

The younger Dutchman rolled some bills into the palm of his hand and passed them to the agent's pocket. "Have a drink on us," he said.

"Not needed," the man said. "Nevertheless…."

The night ferry to Copenhagen breeches the North Sea and leaves many a traveler seasick, especially in treacherous November. Meitner huddled with other adventurous passengers on the top deck, defying the sharp northeastern wind with a sort of rebellious passion. They were going to make it, by God, no matter what lay ahead. The monotonous heaving of the engines finally gave way to a smoother rhythm as the vessel veered from due North to East, finally entering the brightly lit harbor of Copenhagen.

In the glare of overhead lights, the passengers came down the gangway eagerly, looking each way for signs of a greeting party. It was past midnight. The air had a breath-taking quality for many, it seemed, as they braved a wintry rush of air across the water — something akin to freedom. A tall, thin man stood out among the wharf-side greeters. He quickened as he saw a familiar figure coming down the way. "Frau Meitner," he said, "Niels Bohr."

THREE

December 24, 1938, San Francisco, California

It had been a foggy day, but in the late afternoon mists it was now downright murky. The lonely wail of a foghorn hung on the air. Nevertheless, a line of automobiles edged along the Embarcadero from the Ferry Building to the piers southward, gathering for a welcome of an incoming vessel. The Mariposa, pride of the Matson fleet, was due in from Hawaii, on this Christmas Eve.

Suddenly, as the sun settled under the Golden Gate Bridge, a flash of light illuminated the docks. A young woman, hurrying on foot along Steuart Street, looked up at the Ferry Building clock, pulled her light coat around her, and pressed on toward Pier 32. Of course it would take at least a half hour for passengers to disembark, but she wanted to see the ship make its berth. Her best friend was aboard, and she had a surprise for him.

Without more fanfare than a low whistle, a tug nudged the liner into its pier. Gangplanks were down; handlers gathered for the trunks. The first exit was reserved for a gaggle of celebrities and others in first class, well-wrapped against the evening chill. Clark Gable and Carole Lombard caught the newspaper photographers' eyes immediately. From the upper deck of the Mariposa a young deckhand waved frantically, searching for a familiar face. When at last he spied her running along the Embarcadero, he bolted back to grab his duffel bag and make his way down to the gangplank. First class passengers were soon off, second class came quickly next, and an almost equal number of crew — pursers, cooks, waiters, engineers, officers, all except the clean-up gang and the 'black gang' of the engine room —

filed down last. The young deckhand eagerly pushed his way through the crowd to his waiting friend.

"Merry Christmas!" she whispered as they kissed. "You've been away too long, kid. And do I have a birthday present for you!"

Edwin O'Hara had indeed just turned seventeen, yet he had just completed his first tour in the merchant marine — and nobody was the wiser. Leaving a little stubble on his face, letting his hair grow longer, he had successfully passed inspection as an engine-room worker. Fortunately, he had broad shoulders for his medium height. He had boxed in high school and rough-housed with 'Okies' in a valley town near Fresno. He no longer looked like the cherub his teachers called him in school: a little scar under his left eye made that clear. His father hadn't exactly turned him out of the house, as was common in these Depression years, but neither did he object when, high school over, he took off for San Francisco in search of a job. His first paycheck from Matson, earned on his arrival in Hawaii, was dutifully mailed home. It included a brief message: "Dad, you taught me everything I ever had to know about working with the big guys. Mom, you made he a big guy."

But now, here was another reality entirely: the girl who had followed him to the big city. What did she mean, she had some special kind of a birthday present for him? They had never been together, in private, long enough to do more than kiss, and maybe fondle. All those warnings she gave him about not falling for the hula ladies — so much talk. He had seen more bright lights and sex in the bars along the railroad tracks on California Highway 99. On the Mariposa, everything happened "up top," hardly below decks.

Eddie, she called him, even though his mother had insisted on Edwin. He was the same person, either way. So when he called her "Sue," instead of her given name Sulfina, it was an easy bargain. Sulfina Androcles had a certain dignity to it that hardly matched her devil-may-care persona. She was equally his height, fully a woman at seventeen, and played touch football 'with the boys' before the boys knew what hit them. That she would come on her own to the City to meet his ship was accepted in Merced as what every hardy young woman should do. Besides which, she had always bragged about having 'rich uncles' in the City, who would put her up and watch over her for her parents.

They walked hand in hand further south along the Embarcadero, breathless with questions, heedless of where they were going. The first trip: how did it go? Hawaii: what's it like? How'ja get here? What'd your folks say?

"We can walk there, or we can make it quicker, with a jitney," she said. It was the right time of day, as the Mission Street cheap cabs were heading home. They hailed one. "Pier fifty," she called out as they rode off. It was still light and growing calmer as they reached a small cove. The smell of Butcher Town hung in the air. This was hardly the St. Francis Yacht Club, but a fishing boat dock with a scattering of sailboats and motor launches.

"My uncle's boat," she explained. "I got it. Now you run it." The well-oiled wooden cabin cruiser sputtered at first, then glided into the Bay. Soon they were under the San Francisco-Oakland Bay Bridge. All around them, from the West to the City and the East to Berkeley, lights were flashing on. They pointed out to each other the familiar landmarks, the white-washed Claremont Hotel on one side and the stately Fairmont Hotel up Nob Hill, Alcatraz looming before them, finally Angel Island and Mount Tamalpais in the dim background. They were alone as never before, in the midst of a ring of lights from around the bay. It was a lover's lane of a strange kind, on a blanket of water that might as well have been a cloud floating miles above the earth. Sue and Eddie no longer smiled as they looked deep into each other in a growing sense of anticipation and fear. The sexual tension ebbed and waned as the sun finally cast its last rays across the gate. A surprise 'for his birthday' indeed: but were they ready for this?

The sounds of the Bay were the sounds that mariners have learned to cherish in their dreams: the silence of the night included the wash of the incoming tide, the slap of an occasional wave against the bow, the whisper of a wind through the sails of boats anchored nearby. And always the 'clock' of the deep night: faint tinkling of buoys, the cry of seabirds searching for their favored perches, and the occasional splash of — what? — a boat preparing to anchor, a porpoise, perhaps a salmon heading for the Delta. Finally, the lonely moan of a fog horn, its warning so polite as if to be apologetic.

"The only thing is," she confided, "we have to get the boat back before dawn. I told Mom I'd meet you tomorrow. In daylight. That's when the Mariposa docks. And then we'll take a Christmas Day cruise. Get it?"

"But…"

"They don't get the Shipping News in Merced."

"So how about your uncle?"

"Jedediah is a sweetheart. If I tell him we went out on Christmas Day, he'll wink and swear to it on a bible. You know, there are some people who just love to see other people happy. Most of them are uncles…."

He ran the cruiser to a public dock on Angel Island, alongside several other boats. It was a quiet Christmas eve, they could see, with everyone settling down for that long and restful night. And here he was, in a dream he could not have imagined. She had already prepared the bed below decks when he finished tying up and quieting the engines. Easier than driving a car, he said to himself, and this was nothing like the backseat. The gentle rocking of the waves and the occasional slap of water on the launch's creaking sides cradled them from everyone and everything.

"Take your clothes off," she said. "I want to see what I'm getting." OK, he remembered, she had said this before, on a date after graduation at Merced High School, but then it was all bravado. Now it could actually happen. So he stood proudly, confident that in the dim light of the cabin he would appeal to her despite the feeling that his was not the body of an Adonis.

"Now turn around, Eddie," she said.

"What about you?"

Sue rose to her full height, cupped her breasts in her hands, and twirled in front of him. He saw her in that split second of a brain's calculation, in which every perception of sight and smell and sound coalesces into a thought. Her body spoke of hesitation in a way that no voice could utter. Was it just a quiver, a sheet of doubt in the darkness, a wavering, or was it acquiescence and submission without words? The moment hovered in the air for them both, far too ephemeral for either of them to take into account as human beings — yet their instinctual presence as flesh and blood was as real as the flash of light across the water from San Francisco. They were on another planet, for all they knew. They were gripped in an embrace as fearsome as if life around them would fail if they did not hold each other together as one person.

Later in the evening, as revelers began returning to their boats along the dock, spirited toasts rang in the air and an occasional shout of Christmas Eve merriment pierced the fog. Sue and Eddie clung to each other in solemn silence, under the fog of the chatter around them, trusting only in the fitful rocking of the tide. This was their day, this night.

On the other side of the world, where a war had already been planned but not announced, where armies in a show of strength marched at midnight and guns flashed their anger into the darkness, just to display their prowess, where generals paraded into conference rooms and political leaders put on long faces as they talked to reporters, where newsreel cameras followed the lines of ordinary people already carrying their belongings away from the expected battlegrounds, in wagons and on bicycles — on that other side of the world no one could have guessed that two little people in a skiff on San Francisco Bay would soon impinge on their existence.

FOUR

"Don't you believe any little bit of this bullshit! It's impossible. There's not enough energy in the nucleus to break those bonds."

A spindly, monk-like man with a cigarette lingering on his lower lip slapped a folded copy of the *San Francisco Chronicle* against his thigh. His pork-pie hat, sunken chest, and baggy trousers identified him to one and all on campus, who cared to know, as J. Robert Oppenheimer. The thin afternoon sun of winter had already left a chill on the air. His listener was anxious to get back to his office. "Why would they make up that story?"

"That's how they do science these days — by press release."

"This ain't Cal Poly. It's Kaiser Wilhelm Institute," the patient listener argued.

"Kaiser Cement, you mean."

The monk felt alone, for one of the few times in his life. *He* was the one who made outrageous discoveries. *He* was the one who confounded the critics. There was Bohr in Denmark, Heisenberg in Dresden or somewhere, and there was J. Robert in Berkeley. Who were these characters in Berlin who thought they had caused — *caused* — nuclear fission. *Fission*, for chrisakes! The atom breaks apart, like an apricot around a pit. Then the pit breaks apart! It's never been done before — because it frigging *can't be done.*

But the story in the *Chronicle* made no bones about it. Otto Hahn and Fritz Strassman had broken apart the nucleus of an atom — in the lab. Or, depending on how you read it, they had discovered a *fissionable* element. A large element, a great chance it might break down on its own. Who knew what to make of the announcement? Of course they had none of the gear that UC was so proud of, especially the atom-smasher, the cyclotron. Boy, weren't we good at names! *Cyclotron.* Sounds like a twelve-day bicycle race. How could the Krauts get along without it?

Damn those krauts!

A tall bear-of-a-man, still listening but anxious to get away from his chain-smoking friend without offending him, thought the better of leaving without throwing him some kind of bone — something that J. Robert might chew on. He wasn't yet forty, but still felt the senior to the new geeks of atomic theory. But his field was slightly askew of theirs: he was a chemist, not a physicist — though his claim to fame was to have found a bridge between the two fields. Chemistry was about reactions in the lab, between molecules of known powers, right? Physics was into mind games about those invisible, unpredictable, unknowable powers (or shall we call them forces?) in the *ingredients* of molecules — the elements themselves, and their makeup of protons and neutrons and electrons, the very stuff of the almighty atom — except for the nucleus, that inner core of matter, that essence, or so everyone thought, of real things. But this bear of a man, this listener, was not about to let Oppie vent without a corrective, because he was Linus Pauling.

"Maybe you'd be curious to know what structure has to do with fission."

"Structure?"

"Find a better word. These guys are telling us they fissured the nucleus. They broke down the house. The structure."

Oppenheimer liked the Campanile. It was a sort of giant arrow that was plunked down in the middle of the Cal campus, to mark the center of this forum, where one could give speeches to a vast audience, unlike his warren of an office in Wheeler, or in Le Conte Hall. Here he could walk to the chemistry department, just up the hill, or to the student union just south, for a pickup game of bridge. He thought best when he was on his feet. He also thought best when he had someone to challenge him.

"Do they have a clue about this at Cal Tech?"

"I'll be there tomorrow. I'll let you know, kid."

"Linus, why don't you give up this lecture circuit and stick to one place?"

Pauling waved goodbye and walked down to the small bridge under the student union, across to the dirt path that led up to the Faculty Club. More an enlarged cabin than a permanent structure, it held its place like a sentinel of Western defiance under the few old-growth redwood trees on the campus. At the lower level of the disjointed building, the Bernard Maybeck touch was evident: the bar was sedately rustic and as welcoming as a speakeasy. But Oppenheimer made it there before him, almost sprinting by way of the Student Union, and for a reason.

"May I get you one?" the thin man asked, without doffing his hat or allowing his cigarette to leave his lower lip.

"A vokda, already coming. And you?"

"I don't drink. I'll have a martini, up, with just a little ouzo."

"Robert, I'll get you the *Nature* report as soon as I'm in Pasadena. Believe me, they have something. "

"Can you believe it — no word at all today from Lawrence."

"I had a call from Princeton."

"Yes?"

"Not to get your dander up…."

"OK, what?!

"Einstein is positive on this."

"Bullshit!"

"He worked with these guys at Kaiser Wilhelm. He knows what they can do. When Helen and I spent a few days there last summer, he was all worked up about what they're doing in Berlin. Of course, he had his eyes on my wife, but when I could get his attention he actually growled."

"Yeah?"

"That's the way he is. You haven't been through that drill." Pauling sipped his vodka and pointed to the window. "Your buddies are joining us."

"No more Jews are working at Kaiser Wilhelm, right?"

"Not since *Kristallnacht*...."

"So where do they go?"

"If you're lucky, Copenhagen — with Bohr. Or on to Sweden. They've got some great labs outside Stockholm. But who knows how long that'll last."

"But no war yet...."

"Say — if you don't mind talking to an ordinary chemist, what's in your bean about fission?

"I said it already — there's not enough energy in the nucleus."

"Suppose you inject a helluva lot of energy?"

"Throwing neutrons at it?"

"No, no! Lawrence is pushing that. But these great big elements are unstable, right?"

"Uranium, for sure."

"In the right lab conditions, with the right elements in the mix, uranium may just break up. Just in test tubes. Can you believe it?"

"So Lawrence may be accelerating down the wrong path...."

The creaking of the old redwood floors signaled the arrival of guests. There was a time to be outrageous and a time to stick to science. Convivial as it was, the lower bar wasn't the place to do science. Pauling downed his vodka and gathered his collection of lecture notes, books, and rain gear. He smiled broadly at Oppenheimer.

"I'll wager ten to one this Chronicle story is nothing," Oppenheimer said in a parting shot.

"I'll take that bet."

"But why?"

"Because that team in Berlin had a certain woman working on it."

FIVE

May 30, 1939, The White House, Washington, DC

"By all means," the President said, "send me your plans for merchant marine vessels. We'll have our naval architects look them over."

The two British diplomats shot glances at each other before looking back across the conference table. "Um, it may be too late for that," one ventured. "All the signs of war are staring us in the face. Perhaps your government is unaware that this war is going to be won or lost at sea."

Sitting next to Roosevelt, Cordell Hull flinched. "Just a minute here — are you going to lecture the President about how to fight a war. A war that's hardly a certainty —"

Roosevelt raised his hand. "But I enjoy being lectured by such insightful people. You may remember that I was once Secretary of the Navy...."

"Please excuse our impertinence —"

"No apologies needed. When I say 'we'll have our naval architects look at your plans' I mean right now. Do you have anything with you, or can you shoot them over to us? We have a very clever fellow out in California with some ideas about ship building."

"I'll get right on it, Mr. President."

"No, I will. And gentlemen, may I entertain you tonight on board the *Potomac*? I think you'll my little launch convivial to your pursuits."

"We'd be honored to join you. But can you tell us something about this ship builder?"

"Tonight, gentlemen, tonight. Just get your plans over to us. There's no bureaucracy around here, I hope." There was a muted laugh around the table. This was a government by, for and with bureaus.

Henry Stimson, Secretary of War, was not one of Roosevelt's gang of poker players, who were in the habit of assembling on Friday nights on the President's yacht. But this time he made an exception. "Get Henry Kaiser on the phone," the President commanded. "I want to know what he knows before we talk to the Brits tonight."

Henry J. Kaiser was a road builder at first, then a dam builder, a construction man with cement and very large earth-movers, by trade. But he had also his hand in building ships for the United States Maritime Administration starting in the mid-1930s. Through that work and his immense triumph at the Grand Coulee Dam project, Kaiser was well known to Roosevelt. The Great Depression had been weathered by means of massive public works projects. One thing Kaiser understood instinctively was the need for scale in solving large engineering projects. Scale. When Stimson reached Kaiser by phone that May afternoon, Henry assumed it was about bidding on another great public works project. In a way, it was, only of another scale.

The British diplomats were less than impressed when they arrived at the *Potomac*. The gangplank to the yacht, anchored unceremoniously on the Potomac, was of the simplest kind. They had no way of knowing that Secretary of War Stimson had already run the British ship plans by Henry Kaiser's aide at the Maritime Administration. They were also unfamiliar with Roosevelt's sense of humor. As they ducked their heads and stumbled into the narrow cabin of the *Potomac,* they had that familiar feeling they were being taken.

Roosevelt was already well ensconced at the head of the cabin. The aroma of a cigarette wafted over the room, his long filter casually in place. He was shuffling papers, adjusting his bifocals as he shuffled what blueprints hurriedly. When he looked up at his visitors, he said almost absentmindedly, "I like your designs, but I have to give my cohorts the benefit of the doubt. Have a drink, and then let's talk about it."

The British diplomats quickly found themselves in a fen, a situation they were familiar with in their country with a certain Winston Churchill. At least they realized they were in no position to argue. "Mister President, this is a great honor to be in your personal quarters. Yes, we'll have a drink, and to the courage of your country."

"I don't quite understand. Courage? But we haven't shown anything. Yet."

The senior diplomat took the bit in his mouth. "Mister President, you have never made a mystery of your... disability."

"You mean I'm a cripple."

The diplomats looked at each other in disbelief. Roosevelt jumped on their consternation. "The press has been kind to me. So have my Republican friends. Maybe some day we'll have a Jewish president — you know there're some guys out there who would like the public to believe that I'm Jewish...."

Stimson said, "What'dya mean 'some guys.'"

"I love it! Maybe I'm also Catholic. If you listen to the radio, you'll know how far that'll get you."

A porter arrived with a platter of soft-shell crabs, hot butter, and biscuits. His eyes met the President's. "Henry, ask what our guests will have."

"This is really quite enough. But maybe a sherry?"

"Why didn't I know that!? We are so eager to type ourselves. What should I be drinking? Bourbon? Scotch? Actually, a little gin and tonic suits me fine, though I chose Scotch in your honor."

The porter placed Presidential napkins on the gnarled table, wrote briefly on his pad, and reached into a wooden cabinet behind him.

"Do you think, some day," Roosevelt continued, as if in mid sentence a minute ago, "that a Jew will be President, that a Catholic might, or even that a woman might? I'm living proof that a cripple might."

"Sir —"

"Or that a Negro might?" The porter allowed a broad smile to spread over his face, for he was a black man, the color of service in his profession. Roosevelt raised his glass of scotch and gestured as if to toast his steward. But his joviality quickly vanished from his face, as if he had told a bad joke. "Let's hope," he said, "What else can we do?"

After an uncomfortable minute, as the President collected his thoughts, he finally broke the silence: "Let's look at the plans again."

Stimson rolled out a sheaf of drawings and checked a clipboard. He said, "This is only a quick shot, but these are our concerns. As our designers say, you want a packet and we want a cruiser."

"Hmm. You mean to say we've under-designed this?"

"More to it than that. We have to live with the Far East. Not just getting across the Atlantic."

The British diplomats remained silent, as if chastened for coming up short. Roosevelt changed the subject. "This fellow Kaiser, as I've said, has some good ideas. You should go out West and see what he's done."

"We're due back in Bristol next week."

Roosevelt ignored the thought. "Have you heard of the Grand Coulee Dam? It's now the biggest thing on earth. Bigger than the great pyramid at Cheops. This man Kaiser filled that Columbia River with enough cement to take you around the world — I don't know — on a roadway."

"We've read about it. Great job."

"It's been ten years in the doing. But you know something, this guy Kaiser can get things done fast. Let me tell you—"

Henry Stimson could see irrelevance when he saw it. He put down his drink, rose from the table, and went to the drawings he had rolled up on the sideboard. It was as if he had said, "Let's get down to business." But the President was on a roll, and there was no stopping him.

"There's something else about Kaiser you should know. May I tell you?"

The diplomats had no choice. They looked to Stimson as if to ask for a reprieve.

"By building those dams, Mr. Kaiser has come up with a better way to build *ships*."

Stimson saw that his boss was on one of his patented sales jobs. But he didn't calculate what came next.

"You've heard of Joe DiMaggio, haven't you?" There was a long silence. "Please forgive me — this is baseball, not cricket. You still hit the ball with a bat, but then the comparison ends. See, this fellow DiMaggio came up here from San Francisco a few years ago, and all of a sudden he's breaking records. He's an All Star. He's on a hitting streak every time you look on the Sports pages."

One of the diplomats sought to show some concern with the President. "Of course we should know about these sports figures, but you understand we just don't know this country in the short time...."

"Exactly my point. You should go out and see the Grand Coulee Dam. That's on the Columbia, in Washington state. And while you're at it, go down to California, and the Yosemite National Park. I was out there just a month ago, dedicating a tunnel cut right through a giant sheet of granite."

The diplomats were frozen in respect of the speaker. And he knew it. But he persisted to make his point, which came completely around the mountain. "This fellow Kaiser told me one day that the way to make ships is to get rid of rivets."

"Rivets..."

"Yes. Rivets need overlaps. They need heavier steel interfaces. They take a lot more equipment..."

"But, but..."

"Give me all your 'buts.' Henry will answer you."

"What's the alternative, welding?"

"Of course. But high-arc welding. And by machine. Oh yes, the human hand is still there, but everything's rigged up to make it easy."

"Hmm. Let's consider this, Mister President."

"Mister welder," Stimson said. "It's time for some dinner."

As the small plates arrived, the blueprints were moved off the table and the steward brought a bottle of wine to the center. Roosevelt was irrepressible. He was a salesman, as surely for the cabinet as he was for the country.

"There must be something about the air out there," he said, munching on a chicken wing. "They don't do things small."

The diplomats had their hands full of napkins and drinks, and were now faced with another lecture. "But you see, Mister President," the junior of the two said, "we came here to request the building of merchant vessels, not hydroelectric dams."

Henry Stimson knew it was his turn. "Gentlemen, we have some reports to share with you. I think we can convince you that our designs are better for both the Atlantic and the Pacific. Now look — but better, take 'em home and study 'em. And get back to us tomorrow. Is this fast enough?

As supper ended, a few final volleys were sent over the two sides. "This is inspirational, Mister President. Your team is obviously very knowledgeable. We just didn't understand some of your references…"

"If you don't understand how Joe DiMaggio figures into this," the President said, "You'll never understand America."

SIX

September 1, 1939, Lindsay, California

"There's some mail for you, Edwin. On the table."

He knew what this meant: I'm dying to open it. It could be an opportunity or a turn down. But I'm not going to open your mail for you. Not at your age. You're now the man of the house.

Edwin O'Hara saw his father come in from the tractor one scorching summer day two years ago, ask for water, grab at his chest, and collapse on the kitchen floor. He was dead from a heart attack in a minute. The tractor and the five acres of land around it were now in his cousin Ned's hands. Just enough to grow some tomatoes and sugar beets for the grange allotment. Just enough to support the mortgage payments on the roof over their heads. His father had left no pension, no insurance — just the two-bedroom board and batten house. He had been through the 'troubles' in Cork City after the Great War, and signed on to a freighter for Boston to escape the Black and Tan. There, in 1920 on a wintry day at a North End fish monger's he had come face to face with Maria Gabrielli, a young waitress with the warm eyes of a city woman rather than of the dairy maids he had known in County Cork. They took their troubles with them, together, across the beckoning country, following the railroad down at last through the Central Valley of California, finding a farm where they could hope to make something of a life with a new son. This was all I ever asked for, Edwin O'Hara told himself and anyone who would listen, a son of my own to carry the O'Hara name, and even my own given name, into the future.

Maria O'Hara didn't mind at all the pleasant rhythm of her name. It stopped people who assumed she was from the old sod. Change it to 'Mary,' her friends sometimes suggested. It registers better on job applications. It allows you to blend in. Blending in was one thing Maria never had on her mind.

"If this drought keeps up, Ned's gonna lose his tomato crop," Maria went on. She turned on the radio and dialed to the Fresno station that carried news at six o'clock, her regular ritual, picked up from her late husband. "Edwin, are you interested in your mail?"

The young 'man of the house' emerged from the back bedroom with a book in his hands. "I've been studying for the entrance exam." He looked at the return address on the envelope: California Maritime Academy. Maybe there wouldn't be any exam. But the letter read, "We are pleased to inform you that you have been accepted at the...."

"Mom," he said in disbelief. "They gave me credit for working on the *Mariposa*. They're gonna take me!"

"So that trip to San Francisco was worth it all. Call Sue...."

Edwin didn't have to call his girlfriend. She came by most days after school — for she was only a senior in high school at Tulare, just a few miles West. Their meetings were routine now: Susan assumed they were headed to the altar as soon as all the little details were sorted out. Well, this was more than a detail. If the 'man of the house' was going off to school in the San Francisco Bay Area, where did that leave his mother?

Even before her husband's death, Maria had worked in the tomato cannery in the high season of mid summer and at the sugar beet plant in the fall and winter. Without an Army pension or much in the way of Social Security — that new-fangled government thing — there wasn't much left to pay the mortgage on the house. Being a farmer was as about as being a small businessman as anyone could imagine, he'd always said. No fallback.

Now there would be an extra burden — the cost of tuition and room and board at the Maritime Academy. That always came under the decision-making process as 'something will happen.'

Why do you have to go to any damn academy? Susan argued. You've already proved you can handle a shipboard job. But now the reality was clear: just showing up at the hiring hall and being lucky enough to sign on for a trip with the Matson Line didn't mean much for the long term. Edwin saw enough on that voyage to know that an engineer's job or eventually an officer's job was the only way to make some headway in the business.

The letter of acceptance from the Maritime Academy was, however, like a sign from heaven for Maria. This was a turning point, a pathway to another life. She understood instinctively that her life would from now on revolve around her son's. Even before Susan was over her excitement that evening at Edwin's 'paper' accomplishment, Maria was turning another kind of paper in her head.

"We can sell this house," she said with authority. "There's a cannery in Merced where I can work. It'll be a lot closer to San Mateo, or wherever that school is. And I can move in with cousin Sarah."

"What cousin Sarah?" Edwin blurted out.

"There's always a cousin Sarah somewhere in your family," Maria answered with nonchalance. "I'll just have to find her."

In the background, as they talked, and as the evening wore on, the Fresno radio station was playing a live broadcast from Los Angeles of a "big band" performance at a ballroom. The record stores in town were centers where teenagers gathered to listen to new recordings, and occasionally buy a 'single' if someone had the money. The Carnegie Hall Jazz Concert by Benny Goodman and his orchestra, in late 1938, had just come out on two sides as well as an album. Parents didn't 'get it,' the kids said, but Maria did. When the Goodman band came on the air, she stopped the talking and held her right arm in the air as if to enforce silence on the two talkative teenagers.

For a few moments the lonely wail of a Goodman saxophone wafted over the kitchen, a miracle of sound that not Mozart nor Beethoven could have imagined: that in this remote, dusty farming town of the eastern slopes of the San Juaquin valley of California there would be a musical performance of exquisite delicacy over a pine kitchen table.

For a few moments, Edwin and Susan thought back to their idyllic voyage to Angel Island, and the explanations the next day to her uncle, who was hardly unaware of the purposes she had made of his yacht, and the further qualifications to their parents on their return on the train to Tulare and then Lindsay about the discrepancy in time between when they met at Pier 32 and when they managed to get a train home. And in the rhythm of the brass of the Goodman band they felt a surge of the devil-may-care rush of life of going off to a new mysterious… something. The high school at Tulare had everything to offer in sports: all the distances in track, the javelin, the pole vault. Edwin could gauge himself by how fast he could run the 100 better than by how well he could read Chaucer. And now he would have to find another measure, in a big-city space he had only so briefly plunged.

"We interrupt this program," the announcer intoned, "with a news report from the Associated Press. Germany has announced that it is invading Poland, with the intention of regaining its seaports on the North Sea. It appears that Russia is responding to its pact with Germany to also move into parts of Poland from the East. The British Parliament is in emergency session. According to commentators in London, there is the strong possibility that Great Britain will declare war on Germany as a result of its international agreements with Poland and other countries in Europe. More details will follow as news continues to come in. We regret this interruption of your regularly scheduled program."

There was a short silence before the band's music came back in volume to the kitchen of the valley home. In some uncertain way the music no longer seemed to count for much.

SEVEN

October 27, 1939, New York City

The front man at Jack and Charley's 21 knew their guest by sight, as he stepped gingerly down from East 52nd Street into the foyer. The guest's father had entertained his customers in the 'rag trade' here for years — and he tipped well. He was known by that familiar coinage, a 'five and ten' man — five for the maitre d,' ten bucks for the waiter. If there was wine, the steward could count on even more. Such was the value of expertise.

The guest went immediately to the downstairs bar and, coatless even in this chilly fall weather, removed his pork-pie hat in deference to the institution. Before he lit his customary cigarette he nodded at the bartender for his customary dry martini. "I'm expecting three companions," he said with a touch of disappointment, noticing a slim, dark woman at the end of the bar, also with a cigarette. "So three upstairs in about a half hour. Oppenheimer."

Though he was only in his mid 'thirties, there was something childlike about this man, perhaps in his thin blue eyes and finely wrought features. He was a pixie, all right, an illusion he seemed to wish to dispel with the ever dangling cigarette. He would never make a move to engage the woman at the end of the bar in conversation. But he knew from experience at an early age that patience and chance favored the opportunities of the 'special' ones. What made one 'special,' he couldn't define. It was just that everyone knew who was special. The fact that he was a married man, on a mission of great importance — in his opinion — scarcely deterred him from being open to a chance encounter, as he was wont to put it.

The woman at the end of the bar grew in importance to him after a few sips of his favorite drink, especially as no one, at this prime time of one o'clock, chose to sit between them. So in a moment of high expectations — which he had for his coming lunch meeting — he raised his glass even so slightly in hr direction, as if, at least, to acknowledge her presence. This was at least chivalrous, he thought, and even perhaps compassionate. She was nursing a drink. Whom was she waiting for? What tragedy was she soothing?

At this moment two men strode down the stairs to the bar and greeted him with enthusiasm. "Elsa, please join us!" the senior man said, "I'm not surprised you were earlier than us!" At this moment, Oppenheimer's calculation of Elsa's importance to the meeting rose exponentially. And for another reason, as well: she was the physicist in the meeting, he soon discovered. He was embarrassed to remember that he had asked that she attend this meeting. He had simply told the Belgian embassy to make sure that a woman attend the meeting. He hadn't explained why.

"Well then," she said, as they finished their introductions over another round of drinks for herself and Robert, but none for her compatriots, "we received your urgent message and we treated it urgently. Fortunately, we are all based in the Belgian Embassy here in New York. You can understand that Belgium is hardly able to pay any expenses in its current state of affairs." Her Belgian superiors nodded in agreement. They were quite willing to let her direct the conversation.

"All the talk is that Germany will invade France through Belgium, as they did in 1914. So you're in the crosshairs."

"Forget all the talk," Elsa replied. The Belgian diplomats nodded.

"You mean they'll just roll over the Maginot Line."

"Of course. Has any wall, at any time in history, stopped anybody?"

"The Great Wall of China?"

"Try again. The only wall that means anything is human will."

"Which brings me to —"

"First, let's make this clear: we know you want our uranium. What do we get in return?"

Oppenheimer squirmed but tried to match her point for point. "How about the safety of the Western World?"

"Break that down," she replied.

Oppenheimer thought for a minute: he had no authority from Roosevelt or Harry Stimson or anybody else in the Administration to give away something for the vast stores of uranium that the Belgian Mining Association had stockpiled. There was really no reason for them to mine that obscure element — the last in the list of the known 92 elements — except that they had a rich abundance of it. Somehow, someday, it had to have a value. The Belgian Congo was otherwise not very distinct in its mineral rights. Oil, of course. But the 92nd element? It had an ambiguous quality about it: was it really the top of the chain?

"Oppie says let's eat." He made no bones about using his accustomed name to break the ice. "Perhaps after we feed our brains we'll come up with a good quid pro quo."

"But first," Elsa persisted, "tell me why you asked me to join this meeting."

"Just instinct. You have to understand that Manhattan is crawling with German spies. I wouldn't doubt for an instant that they've tracked me here."

"Therefore?"

"Therefore I had hoped this would be seen as just a dalliance on my part...."

Elsa smiled. "Shall we give them a performance?"

Her Belgian escorts winced. Again, the senior of the two men interrupted quickly. "Your point is well taken. Why should we repeat what you already know? I say we leave you two alone to work out the details." With that, he nodded to his companion and the two left without as much as a handshake for Oppenheimer.

"If you think New York is crawling with German spies, you should see the Belgian Congo." Elsa looked around the quiet room. "That waiter, for example," she said. "He's been walking in and out of here every few minutes and I haven't seen him carry a drink in either direction."

"What do you suggest?"

"Just don't pass any papers. If we've been seen already, with those bureaucrats from the embassy, they'll put two and two together. But it was a nice try to make this seem like the usual Oppenheimer socialization program."

"My bad rep precedes me. Sorry."

"Let's get straight to the point. You know the facts already. The Germans are seizing all the uranium they can find in Czechoslovakia. They know there's much better stuff in the Congo. So they send cargo ships down there, and unload tractors. But they're always nosing around for ore to take back. What's this all about?"

"It's about fission. The big difference is between fission in a test tube and fission in a cement mixer."

"Huh?"

"If you get enough uranium in the size of a cement mixer breaking down into smaller elements, you release a helluva lot more energy. Enough to make a bomb." Oppenheimer lowered his voice to a whisper. "Whoever gets massive amounts of uranium can make an atom bomb."

Ten days later, Robert Oppenheimer arrived back at Berkeley, after a quick trip to Washington and a favorite train ride — the Sunset Limited, which took him through parts of New Mexico that he had learned to love in his high school days. At Albuquerque, he hoped he would have time for a side trip up to Santa Fe, but the schedules weren't right. There was a little town up there, Los Alamos, which he had camped around, on horseback, when he was on a summer vacation from high school in Manhattan. Perhaps some day he would make his way back there on a vacation of another kind. There were horses to ride over the horizon, and the horizon vibrated with ridges and swales and vast stretches of open land that stunned the imagination. This was as close to the landscape of a planet yet unseen that anyone could expect to imagine. This is where he wanted his spirit to expand and, just as naturally, to rest.

Any thought of a vacation disappeared, in Berkeley, when he picked up a telegram at Le Conte Hall. It read:

"Dr. Robert Oppenheimer:

Please be advised that we agree with your assessment of the danger of explosive devices being developed from the disintegration of uranium. We are also persuaded by your scientific argument that massive amounts of uranium will be needed to develop a workable bomb. Therefore, in view of the volatile political situation in the world, we are willing to ship ALL OUR STOCKS of uranium to the United States. We assume this will be to New York City, Manhattan. Please advise details of unloading. However, we require that you notify the appropriate agencies of the United States Government of this shipment and provide the necessary documentation."

Oppenheimer was especially pleased by the last line of the telegram, a seeming afterthought:

"We were persuaded in this action by considerations of the safety of mankind. Sincerely, Elsa."

EIGHT

March 20, 1940, Stockholm, Sweden

The letter from the United States, addressed in a Germanic longhand to "Madame Lise Meitner," finally arrived after several apparent side-trips noted in attempted delivery notifications, at the correct office—a small room in the basement of the physics department of a sprawling complex of university buildings. The sender was noted simply as A. Einstein, on Old Oak Road, Peconic, Long Island, New York City, New York, U. S. A.

The postal service in the Swedish capital had not suffered as badly as the rest of the country, as impending war brought back memories of the deprivations of the 'Great War.' At the Manne Siegbahn Institute, the scientific pride of the country, the scientific journals were still arriving on schedule. Primarily this was because most of these journals emanated from Europe itself, including Great Britain—and few from such far off places as the Far East, South America, or the United States. The latter was looked down upon as a backwater country teeming with inventors and merchandisers but sadly deficient in basic science. The 'colonies' sent their sons and daughters—primarily their sons—to study in Europe, "get their tickets punched," and then return to Harvard, Yale, or a few state universities to assume their professorships.

At the Siegbahn, Swedes had seen their share of Americans—brash Americans, they usually called them, as if this were a national characteristic. It was dispiriting to see these foreigners, now including Germans, take over the key positions in chemistry and physics—by their sheer numbers. So it was that when Lise Meitner arrived more than a year before she was hard pressed to find more than an assistant's job at the Institute—despite letters of introduction from Otto Hahn, a phone call from Niels Bohr from Copenhagen, a letter of recommendation from Albert Einstein. It didn't matter: there was little money for male scientists, and 'female scientist' was considered a freakish term.

Thus when Einstein's letter finally found its way to Lise Meitner's desk, she sighed at its manhandled appearance, with official-looking stamps and dog-eared edges. She opened it warily. It read as if from an old friend in her hometown near Vienna, in a German hand quite familiar to any middle-European. Her expression grew more animated as she bypassed the usual formalities and came to the letter itself:

Fraulein Meitner:

Your recommendation to me to look seriously at the attempt by the German scientific community to develop a bomb based on the disintegration of unstable uranium into lower elements, with the attendant release of energy, is something I accept with a sense of urgency. As I have known your work with Otto Hahn for the last decade at the Institute in Berlin, I have no doubt of the reality of what they are calling 'fission.' Your calculations of the energy release based on the general equation $E=MC^2$ are within the ranges I think probable.

I have been contacted by a number of physicists in the United States, urging me to address a letter to the President, Franklin Roosevelt, alerting him to the danger of the Germans obtaining a bomb or other weapons based on the fission of the atom of uranium.

Your confirmation of this possibility, in your letter to me of last month, is clear and well documented. I am only sorry that I do not have access to the same quality of equipment as you allude to in order to make valid these observations. But please rest assured that I will draft a letter to the President of the United States, calling his attention to the compelling urgency of this matter.

Sincerely,
Albert Einstein

The timing was good if the timetable was not, Meitner immediately thought to herself. She was scheduled to leave for Copenhagen in the morning. Hahn and Strassman, his young assistant, who had been credited with his boss for the discovery of atomic fission, had come up against a roadblock. Despite all the signs of imminent war in Western Europe, a sort of dismal quietude had settled over the Lowlands and France. Optimists called it the "phony war" — in which German generals received medals for their efficient march against Poland and Hitler remained unthreatening in the face of a buildup of forces by the British and French along the expected invasion route along the Maginot Line. So there was still a window through which Hahn and Strassman could flee Germany and meet up with Meintner. And she agreed, if only for a single dedicated purpose: "I will build no atomic bomb, and I will do my best to stop anyone else from building one." This was the same answer she gave to a telegram from Robert Oppenheimer, who had the temerity to ask her to come to Berkeley.

The ferry to Copenhagen was quiet, unlike the reverse direction, as anyone who could not afford to leave Western Europe on an ocean liner chose the Northern route. Meitner cared no longer whether she was being tracked by the Gestapo. Yet she wondered how Hahn could risk this rendezvous.

With rare bravado, Hahn had arranged a meeting with Niels Bohr. It was all in line with his work at the Institute. He asked Meitner to go alone to a small bar near the docks, and to wait. Hahn and Strassman then went to a friend's house nearby, where two women joined them. The four went to the bar where Meitner was, by this time, dozing in at a corner table. The two women joined Meitner, and escorted her to a beauty salon. Strassman accompanied the two women back to their house, while Hahn made his way to a street that backed on the salon. At the right moment, he disappeared into a back room of the salon.

"You're much too clever to be a spy," Meitner told him. "Even I am confused by all these games."

"The Gestapo doesn't waste their time on Denmark and Sweden. They hire the locals. And you can pick them out by their haircuts. Always neat. And always looking for more than one or two people. They're probably watching our friends' house right now."

"What if you were... reported?"

"I've been given a priority clearance."

"You mean — to build a bomb?"

"Of course."

Meitner stared at Hahn for a long minute. "You! You have the gall to ask me here!?"

"I know you oppose an atomic bomb —"

" —Oppose!? I'm disgusted with you and anyone who would even think of this monstrosity. Don't you understand —"

"Do you prefer death by TNT?"

"I prefer sanity..."

Otto Hahn was a father of three and a man who had suffered through the Great War, a devastated Weimar Republic, and now the rise of a racist dictator. He was also a shrewd negotiator, perhaps because of all that he had gone through. He now had come to the exact point that he had expected. And he had an answer.

"Are you sure that a bomb is the only outcome from this work on uranium?"

"Hitler no doubt thinks so..."

"So what do you do — end the science whenever it might lead to a big bomb?"

"In this climate, yes, yes, yes!?"

"Would it surprise you to learn that Hitler has ended the bomb program?"

Meitner sighed heavily, but restrained herself from rolling her eyes. "I suppose he issued an edict about this?"

"Goering has taken the funds away — for the Luftwaffe. They're throwing everything into rockets."

Meitner was aware of the rocket program—she had worked on jet fuel at the Institute. A few robot-controlled test flights had already been run. But these were just an extension of projectiles. Bullets on wings. "Tell me, Otto, and be honest. Who's got Hitler's ear on this?"

"Heisenberg. He's moved from Dresden or wherever the hell he is and he's now throwing his weight around at the Institute."

"Just my point. He'll want a bomb. Not a rocket."

"He'll want both."

The discussion was over, as far as Hahn was concerned. He needed only an opening to stir Meitner's interest, and then get what he wanted. "Technical point: the uranium experiment isn't going anywhere because the energy release is too low. After all, we're still doing this just in a lab."

"That's true. Get more uranium."

"That seems like a dumb way to do science. Get a bigger hammer."

"Did you ever think of getting away from uranium?"

"Huh?"

"You read the journals. Lawrence is making bigger and bigger elements in his cyclotron, in Berkeley."

"Yes, I read about that...."

"So you get larger elements, and they're unstable—in a bigger way."

"Like?"

"Plutonium."

A brisk wind whipped around the corner of the salon as an older man and the waif of an older woman made their way out the door. For all the world knew, the science they carried in their minds might as well have been the napkins that dropped from their fingers as they clutched at their coats against the dark.

NINE

June 1, 1940, Memorial Stadium, Berkeley, California

Rugby is an adventurer's game. Just enough of football, with the scoring, yet with a drop kick. Just enough of hurling, with the wrestling, yet a massive charge on the goal. Just enough of "big guy on campus' competition, yet without the crowds. And the beers afterward.... This is why a young man of solid frame, middling speed, and burly arms, a man named George Townsend, liked it enough to choose the University of California over other campuses that did not have rugby on its schedule.

Tackling was hard on the bones this afternoon, in the midst of a dry month in the Bay Area. Mud had a way of encouraging the rough-house spirit, but one needed rain for mud. Still, Stanford was playing on the same field as Cal. So on this longest day of the year, as the score seemed to hover at 21-21 endlessly, Townsend had the good fortune to emerge from a body-piled squib with the ball, spring to his feet, and drop kick the leather through the goal.

The news on this Saturday, however, cast a pall over the beer hall on Telegraph where both teams assembled to 'rehearse' their game. "Did you read where the Germans are shooting right around the lines?" "How much longer will the French try to hold out?" "What happened to the British?"

In fact, at that moment, the British Expeditionary Force, of a half million men, was trapped on a beach in Belgium called Dunkirk. Was Hitler asleep at the switch, or did he hope that the safe escape of the British would make his ultimate enemy more amenable to surrender?

The newspapers were filled with speculation. Among athletes at both universities, the rugby teams had perhaps the most worldly wise. They were actually interested in Europe, because they wanted to spend some time there before settling into the pattern of their parents: get a good education, snag a job with a prospect, get into the right clubs. And only then make the 'grand tour' of the Europe that had given them their cultural heritage.

George Townsend had a particular fondness for the French, as his father had flown in the Lafayette Escadrille, in what was still known as the Great War. Jimmy Doolittle was a frequent visitor at his father's house in Piedmont. But his fondness for the French and his father's friends had failed to convince him that flying was a career. In short, in spite of all the best that parents could offer, in spite of the rush of a major sport, in spite of the parade of young women who recognized him for all the best reasons, he was at loose ends.

With a long summer ahead, and nothing but bad news coming from the war in Europe, George surprised his father that June day to announce that he was going to New York to seek his fortune as a war correspondent. He had a year left to finish his degree. But what was he finishing? The required German literature course. The rudiments of probability and statistics. American history. The early scientists, the late philosophers, the medieval dramatists. What he wanted was the bottom line. In a word, adventure.

"You realize," his father said, "that you just can't jump in and out of school. You have to get a degree or tell 'em why not."

"There are universities all over the world," George said. "I'll bet you learned more in the skies over France than in a sociology class."

"Wow, what a deep thought. Every generation does what they want to, or have to. I was over there to make this place possible."

"Piedmont!?"

"Now don't get funny. Let's say it right. You want a little taste of the big world. OK, go for it. Your mother and your sister and I will worry like hell about you. And you'll send us an occasional card. Maybe an occasional request for money."

George didn't feel quite well over the next month. The sound of even a small crowd in Memorial Stadium had a certain resonance in his psyche. He would be giving that up. And he would be seen by his family as the 'prodigal son' off to the dens of inequity, abroad. It was an old story. Biblical. Predictable.

He would do it.

TEN

The most recognizable man on earth, in this beginning of a new decade, was, like a similar man fifty years before, blessed with a wild tangle of white hair that seemed to spring like radio waves from the sides of his head. It was Mark Twain in 1890, and now Albert Einstein. Thus whenever the eminent physicist walked across the campus, through the medieval stonework arches of the square, from his modest house near the Center for Advanced Research, he was encased in an aura of admiration, by students, faculty, and occasional visitors of all stripes. Thus it was that Helen Pauling waved to him from across a parking lot on this crisp fall day, and elicited an immediate wave back.

The Paulings had been here two years before, as was their accustomed practice whenever traveling through the New York area. Their friendship began at Cal Tech in 1931, when Einstein made his first visit to the Western United States, and sought out this hot seat of science on the West Coast. Ever the showman, Pauling had given a typical lecture to his advanced chemistry class, and had seated Einstein in the front row. A giant construction dominated the blackboard area — put together with wooden balls of various sizes joined by means of wooden dowels. The exact length of the dowels and the angles between them represented actual strengths of the bonds joining the protons and neutrons of the molecule. When Einstein emerged from the classroom, reporters from the major media rushed up to ask him what he had learned from the lecture. "Nothing," he answered. "It's way beyond me." He had no reason to mention that he had learned that Linus Pauling's wife was quite a woman.

Now, nine years later, Helen had good reason to use this brush of friendship for a higher purpose. Her years in a religious family in Oregon and her travels across Europe with her husband had instilled in her an understanding of how the world worked. For the first three decades of the twentieth century, the world had worked by war and threats of war. In Stockholm, she had learned a saying from one of Sweden's early kings, giving advice to his son: "You would be amazed by this: with what little wisdom the world is governed." She was determined to make a change in that depressing formula.

When the threesome had settled into Einstein's modest quarters at the Institute, with Albert and Linus well into their favorite vodka on the rocks, Helen broached the topic that was heavy in the air. "Have you had any answer from Roosevelt?"

Einstein had seen it coming, but not quite so brusquely. "You mean the letter Szilard wrote for me to sign...."

"Yes. Whatever came of it?"

"As I remembered, a brief acknowledgment from somebody on his scientific staff..."

"Vannevar Bush?" Linus interjected.

"That's the name."

"If I recall, the letter spelled out how Germany was grabbing all the uranium in Czechoslovakia," Linus prompted.

"The only thing I would change now is the idea that a boatload of uranium, in a runaway reaction, might be the bomb that would destroy a city."

"What would you change?" Helen asked.

"There are rockets now that can deliver tons of payload. I'll give you a little secret," Einstein said. "I read a magazine published right across the river in New York. Aeronautics News. There are reports of the Germans testing rockets that will make propeller aircraft look like your famous Model T Ford."

Linus poured himself another vodka. "So it's been about a year since you sent that letter to Roosevelt."

"That's right."

"Somebody has to follow up," Helen said. "Can you call Bush?"

"Let your husband do it. One person calling back is a nag. A new person is automatically an expert."

"But we need a compelling reason," Linus protested. "The election is scaring the hell out of the White House. This Wendell Willkie is a persuasive cuss. I'm afraid the Democrats don't want to touch the war issue."

"I think we should have some dinner and let the matter germinate," Einstein said. "Let's have some spaghetti!"

"Eating is celebrating," Helen said with a wink at her husband. " I like the idea of earning your dinner with a decision."

The man with the Mark Twain hair disappeared into the kitchen. "It's not much," he said, when he returned. "Just another letter. But maybe you can make something from this."

The letterhead read, "Manne Sigbahn Institute, Stockholm, Sweden." Helen read it avidly.

"Something? This is everything! She says, 'I took the bomb with me in my purse.' "

"If they weren't impressed by Leo Szilard, and all the other guys, including Segre and Fermi," Linus answered, "How do you think a woman's name is going to phaze 'em?"

"So, Albert, Lise Meitner wrote you to say she's been meeting secretly with Hahn and Strassman."

"I don't know how secretly..."

"But she's saying they have the bomb!"

"That's her word."

"I'll take her word to Washington."

ELEVEN

January 7, 1941, San Mateo, California

The Maritime Academy had the look of a California Mission, complete with low-lying adobe buildings and paths of crushed rock winding through carefully sculpted gardens. No doubt there had been other educational institutions here before this one — perhaps a seminary or a community college. There was precious little developed space in the San Francisco Bay Area for a crash program of the Maritime Administration, as this was, so it was taken over quickly and turned into classrooms as well as playing fields and gymnasiums. If there was to be a massive program of ship building, there had to be an equally massive program of training to man the ships.

When Edwin O'Hara arrived on the campus this wintry day, he was well prepared for adventure. With the slim body of an athlete under his leather jacket, a mop of black hair, and a serious glint in his eyes, he could have been mistaken for a young Jack London. He had been lucky a year before, signing on to the Mariposa, so he had this edge over his classmates. It hardly mattered that his job on that luxury liner was just as a deckhand. He had seen the inner workings of an ocean-going vessel. He was now intent on learning what made those engines and rudders and boiler rooms and navigation systems actually *work*.

Just past his 18th birthday, it was also exciting to free himself from family, as supportive as that family had been. It was the age-old imperative of finding oneself. And now it had the added dimension of proving himself: to his favorite girl, to his mother, and to the memory of his father.

More than he expected from his previous trip to the Bay Area, the public around him was sensitive to the coming sounds of war. The daily papers were now full of the war in Europe. The rapid fall of Paris to the Germans, after great bluster from the French about their Maginot Line, left the pundits wondering: was this *blitzkrieg* for real? Trench warfare was dead, for sure, but was the war of dive bombers and tank maneuvers the end of defense?

Edwin was hardly alone in watching the air war over England as a giant game. Yes, you were going to study ships on ocean, but Spitfires and Messerschmitts were engaged in daily, around-the-clock battles, avidly reported in the media. The Battle of Britain, as Churchill announced after the defeat of France in the summer, was at its peak over the bleak winter of 1940-41. When German strategy turned to bombing London and other major populated areas, instead of strategic airfields, the hand of Hitler's megalomania was revealed. On daily radio from London, American newsmen reported the devastation of urban landscapes. But why? Why this shift from head-to-head combat and, instead, a return to the barbarism of bombing civilian populations?

Instructors at the Maritime Academy used reports from the war in Europe to color their lessons. Firestorms in European cities were weekly fare on local newsreels before every film showing. The campus had a certain idyllic character, but it was hardly isolated from the world. Edwin had seen just a little more of that world than his buddies, but he earned their admiration from having been there before them. When his mother visited him a weekend after his arrival, he impressed her with the confidence he had earned in such a short time.

"I know I worry," Maria said. "But it's not about you. You can take care of yourself. But the world is going crazy." As she hugged him, with her head barely reaching his chin, he noticed for the first time long streak of gray in her pulled-back hair.

"I worry more about you—"

"Merced is fine. I can work there in the cannery, come summer. Right now, I've got a part-time job at the sugar beet plant..."

"I've heard that before."

"We did OK selling the house...."

The talk turned, awkwardly, to Edwin's girl friend. Yes, Maria said, Susan's still in school. She misses you, but won't be able to visit until the end of the spring semester. Her uncle remembers your visit very well. You two are certainly a pair. And, no, she's not pregnant, she blurted out.

"We're on a crash course," Edwin said, changing the subject quickly. "You'll be surprised how quickly we wrap this up. Doubling up classes next week."

"How's the food?"

Edwin smiled broadly. He wanted to say anything but the obvious: it's nothing like home. Miss the favorite casserole. They just don't make bread the way you do. Instead, he confessed. "There's a guy here who really digs seafood. Oysters, Dungeness crab, calamari..."

"All those creatures we never had in the valley."

"Mom, I'm going to sneak you into the refectory."

"Fancy word — but actually I am a little hungry."

Edwin had already endeared himself to the campus cook, so it took only a few minutes for mother and son to find their way through the storeroom and into the kitchen. It was a matter of pride for him — he had been a passive participant in the family kitchen all his life. Now it was his turn to open up a little bit of the world to his mother. In the giant stainless steel refrigerator he spied a bowl of picked crab, with the characteristic reddish tinge to the large legs.

"Edwin, no! You're out of line."

"No, Mom, I'm not going to steal anything. I helped the cook pick this yesterday. I didn't have to. I just wanted to learn how. So just have a taste."

Behind them, a large voice boomed out, "Edwin! Let's do this properly!" And thus plates were arranged, sourdough french bread appeared, along with a scattering of chopped lettuce and a mound of mayonnaise with dry mustard and lemon, and two unlikely gourmets sat down to the best feast that San Francisco had to offer.

As the afternoon sun disappeared behind the San Bruno mountains, mother and son wandered silently through the dappled leaves of the grounds, hand in hand, almost oblivious to families of other students. A dozen or so two-story wooden buildings gave the appearance of a row of barracks rather than an academy. It was temporary, everyone said. The California Maritime Administration was in the process of building something more substantial across the Bay. Under the shelter of 100-year-old oaks, however, the sky never looked more beautiful to two people whose lives had always been accustomed to the 100-degree heat of a small valley town.

"How's that clutch on the car?" Edwin asked as they prepared to say goodbye. "It was slipping the last time I drove it."

"Had it adjusted in Lancaster. Works fine."

"I still don't want you to drive it again. I'll take the train down in June. Tell Susan...."

"Yes?"

"Tell her there's not gonna be any war. This whole mess is on the other side of the world. I want to marry her, Mom. After I get a good job."

"Haven't you told her already?"

"Sort of...."

"Don't be a dumb bunny, Edwin. You sit down tonight and write her a long letter. If I get a letter from you before she gets one, I'll be mad as hell!" Maria laughed the laugh of a giddy young girl as she searched the face of her son, and saw her husband.

TWELVE

June 19, 1941, New York City

Horn and Hardart's never looked better. Even the tables, he observed, were being cleaned up after each seating with the swipe of a rag and a firm toweling. George Townsend had seen the bistros of Paris and Burgundy, the fish counters in Marseilles and the tapas bars in Barcelona, and he was happy to be back with familiar food. He fingered the coins in his pocket as he eyed the windows offering chicken pot pie and lamb stew and egg salad. After ten days on a freighter crossing the Atlantic, he hankered for a square meal and a couple of beers. He tossed his knapsack under a table and settled into an Irish stew: the beers would have to wait.

The cascading collapse of the French armies, in the summer of 1940, in the face of Stuka dive bombers and blitzkrieg Panzer tanks, caught many Americans abroad in a world of disbelief. The withdrawal of the British Expeditionary force of a half million men was considered a victory, and hailed by Churchill as such. All of a sudden the word *werhmacht* took on an aura of unstoppable force. In fact, as Eastman had learned from talking with military experts along the Maginot line, German tanks were mechanically inferior to what the Russians had and even to the American versions, the Pershing, and their 'terrifying' Stuka was no where near the dive bomber under development in Santa Maria, California, by Douglas Aircraft. Yet perception was running wildly ahead of reality.

Townsend thought it funny that the aeronautical engineer producing the only real dive bomber of the war, as it was then obvious, was a man with a nicely Germanic name: Heinemann. He was developing the Douglas Dauntless dive bomber, a bear of a plane, at Santa Monica, California — and he was punching little holes in the plane's wing flaps so that air could flow through in a steep dive and keep the aircraft from shaking itself to pieces. These little anomalies of the approaching war were invisible to the man in the street of mid-Manhattan, where headlines of distant events were secondary to the progress of Joe DiMaggio toward an ever increasing string of games where he got at least one hit. A glance at the Daily News showed George that the native of Martinez, California, Joltin' Joe, was on a roll, already with some 40 games under his belt. To the man in the street in New York, Santa Monica might as well be Martinez, and a dive bomber with holes in its wings might be no more outrageous than a guy who seemed to be able to get a hit every game he played.

But George had no San Francisco-area friends in Manhattan, and tugging at him was a need to connect to something on this, his first day of return after almost a year in Europe. What had he learned? Was he any nearer a career choice? Would it be best just to go back to Berkeley and play some more rugby? He thought it might straighten his thinking to take a walk around the city.

George's first stop was at the Bowery Bank on 42nd. His account was nearly drained from his last days in Paris. He completed the draining and closed it. Now it was up 3rd Avenue, but the Irish bars there left him feeling out of sorts, not even worth a look inside. At 44th Street he spied a fancy name, the Pen and Pencil. It was typical mid-class Manhattan restaurant, with steps down into a darkened bar, where photos of writers were mixed liberally with shots of boxers and ball players and an occasional politician. Suddenly he felt expansive, despite his meager bankroll.

During a slowly sipped martini he began to see the beginnings of a cocktail hour — a feature he had sorely missed in the different time frame of European eating and drinking. He was hardly looking for female companionship, on his sparse means, but before long there was a talkative group of women who clustered over two barstools near him. He had forgotten — it was Friday.

"Have one on me," the woman nearest him said, laughing. "You've been sucking on that glass long enough." He suddenly realized they were in their thirties, and he must have looked like a preppie down on his luck — knapsack, leather jacket, and all.

"But—"

"We're all friends here. Girls night out. Ask Herman."

The bartender nodded to George, and whisked his glass away. "The same?"

George should have been a man of the world by this time. He had seen all the dives and some of the divas in Paris. Yet nobody had bought him a drink there, let alone a woman. So he smiled an inward smile. Yes, it said to him, New York was way ahead of the West Coast, and probably ahead of Europe. He could let the invitation go, or was it an invitation? He decided to open up.

"Ladies, what a pleasure. No gal has ever bought me a drink before…"

"Your first time?" another woman chided.

"You gals are just something else. I got off the boat this morning after a freighter trip from Barcelona. I'm floored by this. This is like a welcome home, and I don't remotely know you."

It seemed as if they were more, but there were only three women gathered along the bar a stool away from him. They were simply dressed and refreshingly 'unpainted.' Whether they were good-looking in the pinup sense was a matter he hadn't thought of. In the dimness of the bar their summer blouses could well have been those of a basketball team after a game.

"Well," he finally said, as his drink appeared before him, "at least let me drink to the beautiful women of Manhattan."

"That's all for you!" one replied.

"May I ask," he said, as he finally composed himself, "where do you work that makes you gals so dolgarned sure of yourselves?"

"Dolgarned?" they laughed.

"Damned."

"We're at the recruiting office. U.S. Army. Heard about it? We see guys like you every day."

"Oh...." George let the conversation drift away from him. He had been a pleasant distraction, and that was all, for this chummy trio. It was time for him to accept their courtesy and stay on the sidelines. But the words 'recruiting office' stuck in his mind. Maybe it was time for him to do something, rather than wait for the inevitable draft notice in the mail. Despite all the campaign arguments between Willkie and Roosevelt, in the fall elections, it was obvious that the United States couldn't stay out of the European war. And if a young man didn't choose the service he wanted, he would be drafted into the army. So his friends back in Berkeley had already opted for the Navy or the Army Air Force. Some had even gone to Canada to join the expeditionary force there, and were already in England.

As the three young women picked up their summer jackets and prepared to leave, George laid down a challenge. "If I show up at your recruiting office, do I get special service?"

"Come on down and see," the woman who had bought him a drink said. "But don't accuse me of recruiting you!"

George looked at her, at her faintly Irish face, her simply combed hair, and saw something he had missed for a long time. It was the plaintive smile in her eyes, as if to say, this is just me. There was nothing more than a flicker of recognition, but it made him say, softly, "I'll be at your office tomorrow morning. Just tell me where it is."

That evening, at the 45th Street YMCA, he slept fitfully. What kind of an innocent was he, to go to a recruiting office on the strength of a chance meeting? But as he gathered himself up the next morning, George Townsend plunged ahead with a decisiveness that surprised even him. At a few minutes after ten, he looked around briefly at the 34th Street recruiting station before realizing that his ephemeral friend from the night before was not in evidence. Was she on another shift? Should he come back later? He steeled himself against disappointment, scheduled a test, which he raced through in less than fifteen minutes, and sat in the reception area waiting for the results.

"Mister Townsend, we'd like to talk with you," the examiner said. It was what he expected. He could tell from the speed with which he cruised through the test that he would receive a top grade. He had done this before, at college entrance exams, at grant applications. It was hardly a test for someone who had finished his course requirements at U.C. Berkeley in three years instead of four. But still the question was open. Did the examiner have a quibble with what some of his answers indicated? He was almost careless throughout the exam, as if he wasn't really interested in the whole process.

The examiner invited him into a small room, shook his hand, and quietly closed the door. He had the look of a parish priest visiting a parochial school. Instead of the expected Army uniform, he wore a three-piece suit and sported a tie that remained in place even on this humid summer day. "Mr. Townsend, we've been looking for candidates like you. Tell me what you've been doing the last year."

George remained silent and stolid. He had never been recruited for a job, never sucked into an invitation. He was unimpressed with the whole apparatus of the recruiting office. It was a cattle car: Here, take this exam. Fill in all your personal data. Sign this disclaimer.

The examiner continued, "I notice you wrote you've just come from Europe. Do you speak any foreign languages?"

"Just the usual bar German…"

"I'm serious. Tell me more…."

"Oh, you know — *noch einmal* — just one more. Oh yeah, I took enough German to pass my Masters exam. At Cal."

"French?"

"*Oui*. That was in high school."

The examiner made some notes on a ruled pad as he continued talking. "You must've had a hectic time in France. Sounds like more than just a spring vacation. Any scrapes?

"I saw the Germans march into Paris. That was enough for me. Weird."

"I take it you like adventure…"

"I *did*…" Out of the side of his eye George saw a familiar figure walk past the door window. She didn't look in. Just as well, he thought. Better just a casual happening, on a strange street in a big city, and never again a second meeting — one that would surely dispel the fantasy of some kind of a friendship. Adventure? What did that have to do with an Army recruiting office? He recalled that old movie song, "We joined the navy, to see the world. And what'd we see? We saw the sea." But slowly it was becoming obvious that his test results and his academics and his travels and his languages were adding up to something in the mind of this avuncular fellow.

"Here," the examiner said at last, pulling open a drawer. "I'm going to ask you to consider using this. It's a train ticket to Washington, D.C. And here's a voucher for the St. Alban's Hotel. It's near our D.C. headquarters. I'd like you to report down there as soon as possible."

George looked at the ticket and voucher in disbelief. He hadn't signed anything. He hadn't even asked what options he had. He leaned back in his chair and stared at the father-confessor.

"Look, son, I've watched hundreds of guys walk through here. It's my job to spot and refer the right candidate for a very special assignment. You're the first one that matches what we're looking for. May I tell you more?"

From the YMCA to Washington, all in one day? George Townsend figuratively hit himself in the side of the head. "Sure. Tell me."

THIRTEEN

December 7, 1941, Richmond, California

Henry Kaiser worked best on Sundays. Everyone's away playing golf or getting ready for chicken dinner, he told his wife — who had little use for either. Helen had already raised her two sons and was happy to watch the glorious sunrise over the Bay from their Oakland home, then tend to her photograph albums and rose garden. There it was: the San Francisco Oakland Bay Bridge, which her husband watched over as president of its construction company — Treasure Island, where he tested his seaplanes — and the glittering windows of San Francisco, where, for all she knew, he was at this moment entertaining either A.P. Giannini, the financier of many of his projects, or even Orson Welles and Rita Hayworth, plotting their next film in the City. For all she knew, also, Henry was just another country doctor — and he even looked like one.

But the shipyards in Oregon and Richmond had done their job, and Henry was "at the shop" in a converted warehouse near Point Richmond. His view was just as dramatic as his wife's. In just a year the Kaiser yards, with help from Todd in San Francisco, had delivered 60 cargo ships to the British Royal Navy, employing that new technique of welding rather than riveting the steel plates of their hulls. The Brits had complained that severe cold might break those welds. Henry's rebuttal was "you're not going to Murmansk with 'em."

The U.S. Maritime Administration had no such concerns. The "C1, C2, and C3" hulls he was turning out were destined for Pacific waters. Everyone suspected trouble was brewing "out there," where a war was going on unabated between

Japan and China and where threats and counter-threats were just the ordinary news of the local papers.

Henry looked over his appointments calendar for December. There was something skewed about Southern California, he thought. They weren't interested in his kind of thought process. Yes, they told him, you've built the biggest this and that, the dams, the bridges, the company towns, the roads and of course the ships. Just keep supplying us with your good aluminum and we'll do the aircraft.

We're going to need cargo planes, Henry lectured them. They're not romantic, but they win wars. You and Howard Hughes, they answered. You just don't "get it." Donald Douglas, Glenn Martin, and Jack Northrup were gobbling up the government contracts for '"fighting machines." But he had appointments with them all, in Santa Monica, before the Christmas-New Years doldrums. He would show 'em how Los Angeles could take away some of that business going to Boeing. At the age of 59, he wasn't ready to sit back and... play golf.

It was ten o'clock on this Sunday, and, as he liked to say, he could fire a cannon down the halls of his office-warehouse and not endanger any living thing. He thought about what Roosevelt had told him: "you're welcome back here any time, you and your ideas." But he needed somebody, just now, to bounce those ideas off. He put down his aircraft drawings and walked out to a make-shift deck. The morning fog had already cleared over the Bay. In another hour or so, he could saunter over to the long wharf and pick up some crab. That, and a little white wine and some sourdough would be the perfect companions for a little contemplation.

The sight of a gray sedan parked at the front gate startled him. The guard waved the automobile through. What was his son doing here on a Sunday? he thought immediately. Junior put in long hours six days a week and always told him he prized his "family day." The Plymouth screeched to a stop just below his deck. Of all the things going through his mind, the words that were yelled to him from his son were the most unimaginable.

"The Japs have bombed Pearl Harbor!"

Father and son stood motionless, staring at each other, for a brief moment, as the words took shape. The mind has many failings, but slow speed is not one of them. In a microsecond, the ideas of treachery, stupidity, overreaching self-confidence, pitiful brazenness, immediate retribution, and hang 'em high flashed through his brain. Before he could speak, asking the inevitable questions of time and place and size, his son ran into the building and up the stairs. "This changes everything," Henry said to him. "It's on the radio, I guess."

For the next half hour, father and son searched the local stations for the latest news. The White House would not issue a statement until an official report was given the President. But the commentary, from all sides, was troubling. How could it happen? Where did the military fail? Why were our aircraft caught napping on the ground? Didn't the Navy know enough to scatter its heavy fleet at a time like this?

But there was no time quite like this.

"Did you call Mom?" Henry asked.

"She already heard it from the Bronsons next door. They were crying."

"They have a son on the Arizona."

"Shit yes."

"I think we'd better go home."

As the day wore on, the Kaiser family, with all its accomplishments, became just one of millions of families caught in the grip of uncertainty, even bewilderment. Yet many were hardly aimless. The radio became at the same time a source of badly needed information and a forum for vitriol. It was a time to be a patriot, it was a time to be a scoundrel. The election of 1940, the inaugural of early 1941, was too recent to forget. Who was this president who vowed never to take the sons of America to a foreign war? Maybe this 'sneak attack' was a setup. Maybe it was provoked.

Helen Kaiser had had enough. "I'd like to go to church," she said. "I know I was there this morning. But things have changed. OK?"

"I'm afraid to say it, but I can't join you. Things are…."

"I know — things are going to be popping. That's the way it's always been with you, Henry."

FOURTEEN

January 1, 1942, Taos, New Mexico

If there was ever a New York City boy who dreamed of being a cowboy when he grew up, it was Robert Oppenheimer. Maybe, his psychiatrist at Oxford told him, this is why "you aren't happy with anything in academic life." Maybe this was his epiphany in Cairo, when he read *Remembrance of Things Past*. Other people were just as frustrated as he was! Ordinary men and women wanted to roam wide and far and not have to take the A train every day to an office in a building on a street that never changed.

When "Oppie" swung himself into the saddle on a Palomino on the first day of the first year of the war, he had chosen just the right place for him to do it. An old Indian village, a Gringo town of less than eight years in the making, a place where supposedly Kit Carson bedded down in a fierce winter on his first trip West. The high country beckoned. This was the country where he and his sickly brother were staked out by their rich parents to a summer vacation as teenagers. This is where they could imagine "anything goes." So here he was again almost twenty years later, with a bedroll and a briefcase, in the 145-acre ranch, Pero Caliente. By god he would at least make it to Santa Fe. There he would ride into town and choose his people—not Washington's people — to create a new town devoted to building a bomb that could end the world. Only no one else knew about this except him. That was self-confidence.

Thank god the military people would arrive the long way around: a train to Albuquerque, an overnight there, a half day's drive to Santa Fe. General Leslie Groves (or was it still Colonel?) would bring an entourage here some day, everything short of the crew that was now finishing off the newest building in the nation's capital, the Pentagon. He was promised that as soon as Groves was satisfied with his engineering masterpiece, he would join him in the West somewhere, to help put together that 'little city' that would tame the power of the fission of uranium.

The project's code name, which Oppie disavowed whenever anyone brought it up, was laughably unscientific: Rapid Rupture. It sounded to him like the name of a Bugs Bunny cartoon. Through his friends Hans Bethe and Enrico Fermi he had heard of the code name the Russians had given to the project: Enormoz. The Russians!? The letter from Einstein to Roosevelt was already being passed around intelligence circles in the world's capitals before a dime had been raised in D.C. to do something in response.

Oppie was intent on keeping the site of his choice a secret. He was pleased to hear that his own name had been summarily thrown out of consideration to head the project — by a select committee in Washington — because of his "leftist affiliations" in California. It was laughable: half the faculty at Berkeley had attended the same meetings, during the Great Depression — that he had. It didn't matter that the Russian Bear was in the process of being gored by the German army, or that British convoys, armed with American destroyers, were on weekly voyages to Murmansk with American rifles destined for ice-bound Moscow. On his horse sloughing through the mild snow drifts of a New Mexican mesa, Oppenheimer was in a world of his own imagining.

His thoughts roamed back to his new son Peter, not yet out of diapers, and his wife Kitty, who had packed his suitcase with a few well-chosen books. One of them recounted the largest man-made explosion yet recorded on earth: It was in Halifax, Nova Scotia, in 1917. A fully loaded ammunition ship, destined for Europe, unaccountably exploded in the harbor, with the power of 5,000 tons of TNT. Virtually all of the downtown area of the port was devastated, and 4,000 or more people were killed. Within a short time of that disaster, even before the end of World War I, the influenza virus that was probably spread by that world conflagration, began to overshadow the power of man-made disasters. Now, however, the dimensions of that tragedy were coming back into discussion. Oppie calculated that an atomic bomb under the same circumstances would be four or five times stronger.

The book was typical of those he received from Kitty. For she was the one that dutifully made her husband aware of the problems of modern society and especially modern warfare.

The lone rider presented a stark picture as his Palomino stalked into Santa Fe late that evening. His pork-pie hat, tilted slightly down on his forehead against the gathering snowfall of evening, cast him as the outlaw he undoubtedly wished to be. He brought his horse to a halt in front of the town's best bar on the square—a fixture in his memory of years ago. He rummaged in his coat for a cigarette, lit up, and swung down from the saddle. There was no rail to tie up to. A fire hydrant had to serve.

"Lookin' for a place to stay," he said to two men leaving the bar.

"Well, sir, try the McKibbin's. Yer standin' in front."

Dorothy McKibbin happened to be in her "town" house that evening, the first Thursday of the month. This was a wake-up from the doldrums of this New Year's Day. It was time to get back to work. When she saw a ghost of a man, as dusty from a trail ride as anyone in the movies, standing and shivering before her, she didn't know whether to kick him out or cradle him like a long-lost son.

"If this's a place to stay, Ma'am," he intoned in his best imitation of a Western drawl, "I'm fixin' to stop here."

She gave him a closer look. There was the hint of a twinkle in the corners of his eyes. But she was no stranger to 'ranch dudes' trying to pass for locals. But the cigarette was real, she could sense. The hat was just worn enough to be real. And the fact that he didn't bother to take it off—the clincher. "My real hotel is down the road. I just put up the drunks here."

"Take your pick," he replied after some thought. "I've got a horse outside that needs some hay and water. And I could sure use a martini...."

Mrs. McKibbin could not hold back a raucous laugh. This was bad theater. Who was this innocent? She stood in front of him and sized him up again. Yes, the smell of seat was real. And that parched look about his lips and cheeks. She could only ask the obvious. "How far you come, mister?"

"From Taos."

"Today!?"

"Yes, Ma'am. You see, I used to come out this way a lot. My brother and I were sent here to school years ago. From New York. We learned how to ride. I came back just a couple of times when I could squeeze it in. But this time, I wanted to make it a full day's ride. You understand?"

"Yes, I do. But, please, sit down and fill me in. I'll call my husband at the hotel and get you fixed up for the night."

Oppenheimer had always believed in the rightness, if not the power, of serendipity. It was almost a model of physics. Linus Pauling had gushed about it in their first meeting, when Pauling explained how he had come up with the structure of protein—well before the war. You see, he had lectured his junior scientist, you always look for the simplest explanation in nature. A protein has motion, in a straight line, as it is formed in the cell. Why not? Then it has to turn in a circle to become three dimensional. So you get an object turning in a circle and moving straight ahead. The result: a helix.

Oppenheimer remembered that lesson, coming from a mere chemist, not a biologist or a physicist. He had found other examples in biology when he visited CalTech. So why not apply it in everyday life?

Dorothy McKibbin could hardly guess it, but she would soon be the direct connection to a little town called Los Alamos. She had seen a man with a mission that was quite a lot different from the missions of the Southwest that the Spanish padres had brought here two hundred years before.

Or was it?

FIFTEEN

January 2, 1942 Richmond, California

If there was one fact about life that Maria O'Hara understood clearly, it was the importance of getting in line first. She had experienced this first hand when her husband had worked his skiff out into San Francisco Bay, and when she had filed for his social security widow's benefits, and when she had applied for the summer tomato sorting jobs at the cannery. This was no different—only it sounded too good to be true:

WANTED: WORKERS IN GOOD PHYSICAL CONDITION FOR DEMANDING, HIGH-PAYING EMPLOYMENT IN THE SHIPBUILDING INDUSTRY. EXPERIENCE NECESSARY ONLY FOR ENGINEERING, DRAFTING, PLANNING, AND BOOKKEEPING. RELOCATION EXPENSES PAID. APPLY IN PERSON, KAISER SHIPYARDS, RICHMOND, CALIF. NOTICE: WOMEN AND PEOPLE OF COLOR GIVEN FULL OPPORTUNITY WITH ALL OTHERS.

The ad had been running in other forms since mid-1941, but since the devastating events of December 7 it had taken on new meaning. Congress had passed new appropriations bills. Kaiser Shipyards was entering a new phase of its life. As was the country.

Promptly at 8 A.M. on Friday morning, the first workday of the year, Maria was near the head of the line that stretched along MacDonald Boulevard near the entry gate of the shipyard. Once inside the cavernous cafeteria that had been converted into a hiring hall, she felt quite at ease. The people around her were "her type." Here was little that was different from the hiring halls she had easily navigated for summer work in the canneries. A physical test? No problem: she hadn't needed eyeglasses at any time in her life. When it became her turn to read a chart, however, she saw something new: a "hand-eye" coordinator, they said. As a line dropped down on a well-lit screen, she was asked to move another line quickly from the right or left side to coincide with the lighted line.

"Perfect," the tester assured her. "Now let's do the strength test."

Within an hour, Maria found herself in an office, going over printed forms, and signing her name and answers to questions that made her heart leap. Where do you wish your weekly employment checks to be sent if you are not able to pick them up at the central office? Where may we contact you in an emergency? When can you begin work?

Maria went to her car in the parking lot and wept silently. In one breath she wanted to telephone Edwin at the Maritime Academy, and burst out with the good news. Then she held back: would this disturb him and his studies? He was near the end of his term. He had, at most, another semester to complete his training. Would he take this impulsive action of hers as an "act of sacrifice" that all sons hate? Or would he realize that she simply wanted a better job?

She sat in the car for several minutes, sifting through the hand-out sheets from the employment office: copies of all her signed papers, schedules for the coming training program, lists of places to stay. Why am I sitting here? She suddenly asked herself. Here I am right on the very edge of San Francisco Bay, and I'm locking myself in a car.

Maria soon discovered that she needed a badge, which she would soon be issued, to get through the main gate. But she walked as far as she could in the parking lot to orient herself. Even on this bright day, as the morning fog was burning off, there was a grayness about everything. Cars drove in and out, and buses with the name "Kaiser" emblazoned across their sides were everywhere. Yes, it was true, she was told by the man who interviewed her: Henry Kaiser had purchased an entire electric transportation line, from a New Jersey company, and shipped it here to Richmond. It was running now between Berkeley, where there was plenty of housing, and the Richmond shipyard.

This guy was thinking of everything. Including women. Including the seven-day work week.

When Maria reported the following day to the yard, she was 'herded' to the 'indoctrination center.' You can work tomorrow, Sunday, if you wish. The Kaiser Company respects your religious duties. But if you choose to work, please do not feel you are more patriotic or more in need of take-home pay than anybody else. The message was clear: this was a company where somebody gave a thought to the workers.

Maria was pleased with herself for not calling her son to announce her new job. She would wait until she had something 'under her belt' instead of just gushing. With that simple thought, she sensed, for the first time, what it meant to be treated as an equal bread-winner. If it takes a war to make this happen, she thought, it just shows how bad a fix we've been in.

As the next week drew to a close, she had the perfect thought to pass along to her son. She didn't have to rehearse it at all. It was there all around her and obvious and thrilling — at least to her.

"Edwin," she said, "I'm living in a two-room shack in Berkeley with a friend I met at the shipyard. A woman who works with me."

"Mom...."

"Kaiser shipyard. I'm doing welding. These big steel plates swing down in front of me, and I move them together, grab them with clamps, and then weld then with a gun."

"But Mom! Where are you calling from?"

"Berkeley, I said. Now don't get upset with me. I just went there and applied. And it's the best job I ever had."

There was a long silence. Then a laugh, then two laughs, together. "If I didn't know you better, Mom, I'd say you'd been drinking. I'd ask you to tell me all about it. But your nickels would run out. Just tell me: when can I come visit?"

"In Berkeley? No way. I'll take a day off and come down see you. OK?

"When?

"Tomorrow, Sunday. My religious holiday."

Edwin hung up as time ran out. My religious holiday? My mother has never had a religious bone in her body. But what does a son know?

SIXTEEN

February 1, 1942, Stockholm, Sweden

Thank God for the midnight sun, or the lack thereof, George Townsend sang as he hefted his bags along the docks where the train-ferry from Copenhagen had deposited him. If he were to be a spy, he might as well have the cloak of darkness. The crumbling buildings of the *Stortoget* were just what he wanted. A place to play the Yankee student, mixed up in the time warp of war. The Germans had swept through the Low Countries and taken up residence in Paris. The Brits were happy to have saved their Expeditionary Force from annihilation at Dunkirk. And the Scandinavians, like the Swiss, were happily sitting on the sidelines. Why would you want to occupy us? It would just be more trouble! Besides, there has to be a sidelines somewhere, where the ball boys can run in and retrieve errant shots and where bankers can entertain their clients. And where spies can practice their craft.

George soon found a likely workingman's bar. The regulars looked him over for just a moment, then went back to their beers. Surprisingly, there were a number of young women, clustered together, enjoying their aquavits. Ah! It was a Friday, George realized, and the idea of working on Saturdays had vanished from this liberal paradise some time ago.

As his eyes grew used to the light, George saw that he was hardly the lone visitor in the after-work mix. He had little briefing on what to expect here, but it soon became clear that the Germans, if not the Gestapo, had made their presence felt. Well, of course! This was the purpose of neutrality. And who was to say that the long-standing German custom of making

Stockholm a vacation mecca should end for such a silly thing as war.

George stayed at the bar, nearest the table of chatting young women. Soon he found himself apologizing for dropping his duffel bag near their table. It would not do, of course, to ask directions overtly — to the National Science Academy where Lise Meitner was working. Yet he had only a day — the next one — to accomplish his mission. Thus, he argued to himself, any indirect help would shorten his task. The city was indeed a beautiful show of water working with land — much earthier than the San Francisco Bay of his home. Here the waterways seemed to pop up everywhere, and the vast Baltic beckoned mysteriously beyond.

It seemed rather odd to George, accustomed as he was to bars in Berkeley, San Francisco, New York, and Washington, D.C., that the young men hoisting their beers with vigorous sporting commentary seemed it a sort of chivalry to ignore the women. Perhaps he could break the taboo. Perhaps as the innocent.

"Please excuse me," he ventured. "Any ideas for a room tonight?"

It was just late enough in the evening for one of the young ladies to seize on the same sense of savoir faire. Fortunately, she was aware of American English. "I have a most wonderful idea," she began, to the delight of her companions, "but I'll have to look you over first."

"May I buy the table a round?" George offered as the best riposte he could muster. There was now no denying he was typed as the rich no-good American tourist — but dark haired and muscular.

"You won't get away that lightly!" another woman broke in. "Hey, join us!"

George could sense at once a break in the atmosphere in the room. So, this new guy got away with that? What's he got? Blundering American tourist…. He decided to make something of it. Everyone knew who he was, or did they? Why not make sure they knew he was just a dumb student?

"Hey guys," he said, "I got trapped here. I'm supposed to study at the Institute. So it's all up in smoke. What do I do? Go back home?"

"Go back home, Yankee!"

"Shut up. Let him speak!"

"Look, I'll check in and say I studied, OK?" With that, George got up from the table, moved back to the bar and took a quick gulp of his beer. He had caused enough ruckus already. Yet one of the young women pulled away from the table and joined him at the bar, as if to apologize. They raised their glasses in a toast. Thanks, he thought, but he knew he should have said it.

"We meet here every Friday and talk about our lives, right? Then we go back home and read Jane Austen. Yes, even here. I'd rather spend some time with a guy like you."

Holy smokes! he thought. She was not the darling of the group, and maybe had a few years on him, but she had that twinkle in her eye that spoke of adventure. They were all striking, each in her own way, he realized. They all had the clean look of athletes, and at least tonight without lipstick or eye shadow. That this woman would engage him like this scared him. He knew he couldn't answer too quickly, and too late would end everything. He simply leaned over and kissed her hand.

And I'd definitely rather spend some time with you, he said to himself. So they took up separate seats next to each other at the bar, with the complete approval of the "sisters," and began to talk. A second beer, a second aquavit, and there was so much family history bandied about that grandmothers and grandfathers gathered on each side, if possible, could not have filled in greater detail. Yes, of course, the rest of the male patrons at the bar, especially the Germans, were jealous of this instant liaison. Yes, they resented the American. But of course, that is all he was, and he was playing the role to the limit — just an American on a college fling.

George had just made his most important statement as a member of the OSS. And he had made a social commitment that spies are not supposed to make: to get involved. Finally the moment of truth arrived.

"I know you'll be gone in the morning, and you'll never return. I realize you'll never feel you have to call me, or even give me a trinket as a remembrance. But what if you give me just one evening? Huh, soldier?"

He looked carefully into her eyes, and caught a faint twinkle of abandon, as if she had just lost a lover to another and needed the redress of a chance meeting. Her mouth never wavered from a plaintive smile. He smoothed his hair back as if to clear his head, and whispered an honest "yes."

All the usual rationalizing raced through his mind: this will confirm to everyone watching that here, indeed, is just another reckless American on the prowl. This will keep the German watchdogs confused. Perhaps this lanky Swedish lass may even have some advice on how to navigate the system.

"We're going to get some air," she announced to her friends, with a wink. Before George could stammer an apology for plucking her from their company, she put a long finger to his lips. "He's a meteorologist," she explained. "He studies wind and rain and… air."

They stood outside the bar for a moment as if to set a course. "Let's see who follows us," she said. "I don't know why you're here, but I think you'd rather not be followed."

After several blocks of brisk walking, she grabbed the back of his coat and pulled him into a doorway. "Do you like playing spy?" she asked with a toss of her rich mane of hair. "Go ahead, mess it!"

George reached behind her head and cupped her face to his, then kissed her full lips with an ardor that at any other time in his life he expected to be rewarded with a slap. Instead, she dug her arms into his back as if clinging for dear life. "Do you know how much I miss someone like you?" she murmured. "A real man—someone with fire between his legs."

"You're right out of a movie," he stammered. "Something by Hitchcock. You know, The Thirty-Nine Steps. Foreign Correspondent—"

"Oh shut up. Do you want to make love to me or play the intellectual? Huh, you red-blooded American stud!"

"Gulp...."

"Don't play the innocent. Let's go fuck!"

George Townsend grabbed both her hands and pressed them to his face. "You are such a romantic!" he whispered, thinking all the time about playing rugby and winding his arms around this well-muscled animal of a woman. "Lead me to my doom.... But first, tell me your name again."

"I never told you at all, silly. Maria. Maria Patricia Holm. They call me Petra. You know, like a rock...."

It was all George and Petra could do but skip along the curving street, away from the docks, that lead up to a tree-lined lane. If they had one thing in mind, all of a sudden, they were hardly the first on a wintry night in a strange city like this. Petra's grip on his hand wasn't the wisp of a femme fatale, George kept telling himself. But Wild Bill Donovan's words kept ringing in his ears: those German whores know the ropes; they've been through the worst of times; they know all the angles; they can play angel one minute and Salome the next; they'll outdrink you, outfuck you, outlast you; don't think you can outplay 'em in bed just because you can outplay anyone on a rugby field. But Petra's hand gripped his with a female urgency he had never felt before—a wish to have him, full bore—as she sprung open a lock on a tall, carved door and pulled him up a flight of stairs to another stately door. Inside, the sputtering of a gas heater threw flickering light up to a high ceiling. OK, he said to himself, now it's all in. Either the Gestapo agent appears from the kitchen with a well-polished Biretta or I'm in for an evening of exploration of the limits of debauchery.

"So—now you know," Petra blurted out. "I can't get a man to satisfy my tastes. See, no one here. Shall we start with a drink? Scotch or bourbon?"

"Bourbon? I thought—"

"You thought! Do I have to draw you a picture? I want a cowboy to rope me, OK? And cowboys drink bourbon!"

The tease is over, George knew. I'll let her undress me. Meantime, I'll make her beg a little. They toasted their sudden friendship with their eyes as much as with the bourbon. Then George carefully, deliberately, removed her clothing with a kiss on each piece. He reserved her silk stockings for last, playfully wrapping them around her wrists, which she had compliantly gathered behind her back. "Tighter," she begged. "Don't you understand? I want to be helpless before you...."

"I think you need a whipping," he volunteered gallantly.

"You think I'm not hot enough already?"

"You are. But I think I'd like it—" He removed his belt from his waistband and gave a crack on the kitchen table.

"Anything, but please don't hurt me. If you don't tie my legs, however...."

George was well beyond rational thought. He remembered Wild Bill and volunteered, "Now who's being the intellectual?"

The evening turned into deep night, and deep night into early dawn. George was still asleep, exhausted by everything he had learned from the Karma Sutra, when Petra entered the bedroom with coffee in two tall cups. She handed him some bills. "Be a dear and go down to the local bakery for some buns," she asked. "It will help if you're dressed like anything but an animal."

When George stumbled out the door and down the stairs, he made sure to grab his backpack, fumbling with it as if not sure of what he was doing. "I'll be right back," he blurted. "You are so beautiful! Beautiful...."

Petra smiled after him and immediately dialed a number. "Hubert? Yes, I think I stumbled onto an American up to no good. You can tell them a mile away. I would guess he's smart enough not to come back with the pastries I gave him money for. But he's an easy target. Tall, blue jeans, peacoat, three-day-old beard. Nice black hair! You know, the collegiate type. He's headed for the Institute, all right. I got that out of him last night. No, I did NOT have all that great a time in bed. You're jealous?! You men never get it. He's probably not much of a risk, but one never knows. Have him killed."

SEVENTEEN

February 7, 1942, Tijuana, Mexico

They set out to find the dirtiest, dingiest cantina in this most derelict of towns. They wanted to know the worst, taste the worst, feel the worst. They left their parade whites behind in order to leave their white faces and white souls behind. They were looking for trouble even as they bragged about looking for something they weren't getting from their girl friends across the border. And now they had found it, as the girl with the demure look of a Madonna began removing her dress from the top down, and shaking her hips to the staccato rhythm of the bongo drums and the blare of the single horn player who seemed to be playing either taps or reveille.

"Jesus!" the youngest of them said. He threw back his Margarita and held up the glass to the waitress.

"No mas!" she yelled, teasingly. She pointed at the rest of the glasses on the table and quickly got a nod from the other two for another round. The young men had their eyes fixed intently on the woman playing her body up, down, and around the pillar in the middle of the room. She reached up to a gourd hanging from the ceiling and feigned hanging from it, her face strained in spiritual ecstasy as if she were Joan of Arc being burning at the stake, and imagining that she had no earthly control over the flimsy blouse falling off her breasts.

"I want some of that," the youngest man said.

"Calm down, sailor. Wait your turn!" the lanky Texan advised. "We're going back to the base together." The third man at the table wiped his forehead and pulled at his moustache and peered around at the other tables. They had gone beyond the usual tourist venues. They were the only white faces in the hot, low-ceilinged room. They were the only ones passing dollars around like napkins. They were the only ones staring hungrily at the saint on stage.

"You know, guys, I don't like this," the man with the moustache said. "Keep your money in your pockets." Officers all, they had come from towns in Missouri and Idaho and Oklahoma, and gone to Pensacola, and earned their wings, and shipped across the country to the dream of every young man: young women hanging on their arms and swimming in the blue Pacific from white-sanded beaches and sipping cocktails in grass huts on Catalina Island. The war had come, but their call hadn't. So they spent their time dropping bags of sand on rowboats and trying to land their Douglas dive bombers within lines drawn with chalk on an asphalt field. The closest they had come to an aircraft carrier was the sight of a flat top miles off the coast, probably arriving from the East Coast through the Panama Canal, heading north. All they knew were rumors. The aircraft carriers had survived the catastrophe at Pearl Harbor. They were getting ready to take a crack at the Japs. Any day now....

The youngest man laughed. "What's a matter with you guys? I think she wants to dance." He got up and staggered over to the spellbound stripper at the center pillar.

"Senor!" a large Mexicano commanded. "No!" It was a word with resonance in any language.

"Who says so?"

"No, senor!" Four men at the large man's table pushed back their chairs as if to add punctuation to the command. They wore serapes. The horn player and the drummers stopped as if a radio suddenly went dead.

"Sit down, Junior!" The man with the moustache commanded. His partner winced and held his breath.

"Fuck you!" the young man said, and as he reached out to grab Joan of Arc a hand that he never saw came down across the back of his neck. He pitched forward onto the sawdust floor. His buddies jumped to their feet and rushed toward him, but it was too late. The large Mexican caught his stomach with a sweeping kick, as good as a crossing pattern on a soccer field. The mustachioed American turned to put a headlock on the Mexican. Unlike barroom scenarios in Hollywood movies, there was some sweaty wrestling and clinching and shoving, and then it was over. The braceros had won their honor fight without hitting a chin with an uppercut or even a punch in the nose. The Americanos accepted a quick thrashing, and called a truce. Enough!

Still panting from their dust-up, the Texan and the man in the moustache assessed their losses. Their amorous younger comrade slumped in his chair. There was little physical damage. Maybe a broken table. The adventure south of the border was over. The Texan walked to the bar and threw two twenties in the direction of the waitress. She looked at the other tables in the room before she picked the money up. The men in the serapes nodded their approval.

"Where the hell's the car?" the lanky Texan said. Unlike the man with the moustache or the youngster, he had a square jaw and black hair to go with his deep brown eyes. He held a handkerchief to the young man's head, where blood continued to gush from that most delicate bone in the forehead — just below the eyebrow.

"It's a good walk, pardner. We didn't exactly follow a straight path to get down to this God-forsaken dive…. " They stumbled outside. The crisp night air was just what they needed.

Suddenly a familiar wail broke the silence. A jeep spun around the corner. It was clear from the armbands of the driver and his passenger that they were not a rescue squad.

"Military police!" the sergeant next to the driver yelled. "What's all the ruckus about?"

"It's over, sergeant," the Texan answered. "Just a beef."

"Oh yeah? That's not what the bar owner said."

"What the fuck is this? Our buddy just got cold-cocked for looking at a girl."

"Hold your lip. Let's have your papers."

"Sergeant, sir, we're officers from Naval Air Station, San Diego. We're just out celebrating —"

"I said let's have your papers. Officers…"

The lanky Texan removed his handkerchief from the young man's forehead. He wanted to ask what business is it of a bar owner in this sad excuse for a town to get the MP's on the phone over a stupid bar argument. He wanted to ask if anybody cared that their buddy was hit in the head pretty bad. He wanted to say a million other things about the army versus the navy, but he knew, even as drunk as he was, that arguing with the police never pays. So he fished through his wallet, as did the mustachioed airman, to find their U.S. Navy IDs.

"What about him?" the sergeant asked after inspecting their cards.

"Fuck you," the young man whispered.

"What did you say?"

"I said fuck you! It's two months after Pearl Harbor and our buddies are getting killed on Wake and the Philippines and you are fucking asking for our papers?"

"Oh, so we have a history genius on board? Sorry sailor, but you're goin' to the brig."

The Texan held his hands in the air. "Can I have a time out, please? And I mean that, kid — shut your fuckin' mouth up."

A group of Mexicans leaving the bar sauntered closer, hoping for a fight. There was nothing like a shouting match to grab attention. The MP waited for a minute before answering. "OK, but make it good."

"Thank you, sergeant. Our young partner here has just gone through a very bad time. You see, we're dive bomber pilots, and we've been training 12 hours a day for the last two months. And he just lost a good buddy…."

"This better be good. I aint got all night."

"We were formation flying, with our cockpit covers open, and his plane came too close to the one right under him, and he cut his buddy's head off."

"Jesus, what bullshit!"

The man with the moustache broke in. "It's all true. And he had to go to the morgue this morning and identify his buddy — without the head."

The MP looked at his driver as if to say, are you taking all this in? "OK, so you say he's emotionally screwed up, is that it?"

"He's got a letter in his pocket from his buddy's mother. To his buddy. To her son. See? And he's got to answer her, and tell her what happened. She works in a shipyard in Richmond. He's the only living relative. Only he's dead."

"OK, OK! Show me the letter and I'll bite."

The young man pulled his wallet from his hip pocket. He slid his Navy ID from its cover, then pulled a tightly folded paper from his shirt pocket. He handed them both to the sergeant. The Texan gave the young man a hug.

The MP snapped his flashlight on the letter, read for a minute, then quickly handed it back. "I guess you officers never seen blood before, but you better get used to it. Get the fuck outa here. Straight back to camp. And teach the kid some manners, see?"

One hour and a half later, after a long walk to regain their senses, the three men pulled their 1938 Lincoln convertible through the guard shack at the U.S. Naval Air Base in San Diego. It was just barely before dawn, so that lights from the city had yet to brighten the night sky. A full moon cast its presence over the two-story wooden barracks and the deserted assembly ground of the base. The three men sat for a moment in the car, in a kind of penitential recollection of the events of the day. The youngest continued to hold a handkerchief to his forehead, but at least he was coming around. Before going to their rooms, they talked about how they could all work on a letter to be sent to the Richmond shipyard. To the mother of the son whose head was chopped off by one of his buddies.

Then, one by one, they noticed a familiar white package sitting behind the screen doors of their rooms. That meant only one thing: an order. The Texan opened his packet first. It read, "Report to command central at 0100 08 February with all gear. Air wing SDB-3, 1215, to deploy to Honolulu. Emergency Status."

"That's tomorrow," the kid said. "We finally got our wish."

"Today, you mean," the Texan drawled.

"What'll we do with the Lincoln?" the kid continued. "Why don't you give it to your fancy girl friend at RKO? You know, the one who don't put out…. She'll hang on to it for ya. Hell, this war'll be over in two-three months. Those puny Japs'll come crawlin' for mercy…."

The man with the moustache and the Texan looked at each other blankly, as if to say, This is what the American people believe. This is how we got into this mess. This is what we have to deal with.

"Well?" the kid said. The chill of an early morning fog now hung over the base. The Texan took the car keys and threw them in a long, looping arc to the flag pole at the center of the parking lot.

"You've got a letter to write. Let the next guys have the car. Ten to one none of us will be back here."

EIGHTEEN

February 16, 1942, Los Alamos, New Mexico

Oppie sifted through the afternoon's mail and stopped suddenly when he saw the familiar stamps of Sweden. The sender's name, clearly lettered on the envelope, was Stanislaw Ulam, but he knew this was impossible. The Polish mathematician had made a name for himself at Harvard at least four years ago. If memory served him, Oppie thought, he had applied to Berkeley and wanted to get into the Radiation Lab. He slit the end of the flimsy envelope with his pen knife and extracted an equally thin piece of paper. It was dated in mid January, a full month ago. Some news about Lise Meitner?

He shook his head in disbelief as he scanned the carefully penned document, as neat as an algebraic equation. It began:

My dear Professor Oppenheimer:

As an admirer of the game of chess, I forward you herewith a game I played recently against world champion Dr. Alexander Aljechin. It was at a simultaneous exhibition in Berlin, sponsored in part by Herr Hitler. It was conducted at the Kaiser Wilhelm Institute in honor of the eminent physicists who have achieved scientific acclaim in the discovery of nuclear fission. I was able to catch the world champion in a devilish trap, but of course he was playing thirty other scientists at the same time:

1 e4 e5 2 Sf3 Sc6 3 Lc4 Sf6 4 Sg5 d5 5 e:d5 Sd4 6 c3 b5 7 Lf1 S:d5

8 c:d5 D:g5 9 L:b5+ Kd8 10 O-O e:d4 11 Df3 Lb7 12 D:f7

….and at this point, when I played 12… Sf6 the world champion suddenly realized his queen was trapped, his bishop was en prise, and he had to tend to a threat of mate on the move. In honor of the occasion, the doctor had not been imbibing his favorite vodka, so he realized the need to resign at once. How fast things go in Berlin! But breaking up in twelve moves?

Please do not respond to this letter, as I will be finishing some mathematical calculations here in Sweden, where I have been allowed full diplomatic courtesy by the German consulate. Perhaps you would wish to visit me here, if the U.S. government allows you the same courtesy.

Science uber alles!

S. ULAM

Oppie looked again at the envelope. Yes, it was addressed to him at the University of California. There was no obvious sign of steaming open the flap. But, of course, it was rumpled in the process of moving through many hands before its final arrival in a canvas mailbag from Berkeley. Then he looked at the signature at the bottom of the sheet again. Holding it up to the window, he could see, ever so lightly, the "L" and the "M" of the proper name ever so slightly emphasized. If this is a coded letter, he thought, it's rather amateurish.

Hmmm. Science uber alles: SUA. Delete from S ULAM?

Oppie thought back to what happpened a bare week ago, as he tossed another cigarette butt off the deck of his woodsy Berkeley home, fully aware that this had been a particularly warm winter and the brush around his neighbor's home directly below was Autumn-dry. He could just see the back of the Claremont Hotel over the next ridge. What a fine fire it would make, he thought. But his mind wasn't on the dangers of a hot, dry wind. And, after all, the Berkeley fire department came on cue to that little blaze. The big issue was the biggest fire man had ever seen. Why in hell won't Grove ever call? He asked himself hourly, until the call finally did come, and here he was in his chosen milieu.

But what's this about: "How fast things go in Berlin"? Yes, it was a short game — unheard of for a world champion to lose. Nuclear fission is, of course, on everybody's mind. "But breaking up in twelve moves"?

"Jonesy! Get me a line to Harvard! I don't care if it's eight o'clock there. Somebody must be working...." he yelled, as if on an intercom.

A statuesque woman in baggy trousers and a sweatshirt threw the door open, as one had to do in this barracks-like building. The virtually windowless room, with its cavernous, pipe-filled ceiling, had been a boiler room or a laundry. Now it was lined with blackboards, file cabinets, and wooden racks for filing books, magazine, and reports. "Pick it up," she said, softly. "I think I've got the janitor."

He picked up the phone and composed himself. "Pardon me, sir," he said intently, "this is an emergency. Can you, or anyone else, there, find a gentleman named Ulam? Yew-lamb. Or maybe Ooh-lamb. This is the federal government."

"Well this is the library," a hushed voice came back. "Exactly who is this and why are you calling?"

"Well, yes, I do work for the federal government. I'm in New Mexico and I've got to find Mister Ulam. Would there be any way for you to help me?"

Jonesy smiled her approval of his new approach. She scribbled on a scrap of paper and handed it to Oppie. "Does he have a library card?" He blurted it out dutifully.

"At any other time I would have said it's none of your business," the librarian replied. "But this is mid-terms and I'd kill to do anything to get through the next hour here."

In a few minutes she had a complete answer. "I can even tell you he checked out a book last weekend. That's right. Stanislaw is his first name. Some hand-writing. Is he an M.D.?"

"Jonesy, let's have a martini," Oppie said as he banged the phone down triumphantly. "Even though the six o'clock bell hasn't rung."

She glanced at the mail spilling out of the duffel bag she had delivered earlier. "Are you certain there's nothing else in there to get your attention?" She smoothed back her auburn hair and threw a pack of cigarettes across the desk. "Why don't you make the martinis?" she said. "I'll see if we can't get some heat down here. My ass is frozen."

Robert Oppenheimer gathered his lean frame to his full height, just under six feet, as he gauged it, and went to an antique sideboard under the only wide window in the room. A cigarette dangled from his lower left lip, unlit. It didn't do to have ashes in the martini. But he did believe in a modicum of vermouth, and he had a special one from Verona. No stuffed olives or pickled onions. Maybe a lemon twist or even the zest of one on the stirring spoon. His secretary, or major domo, as he fashioned her, ate the onions separately, and preferred the gin on the rocks. He liked the martini in a crystal clear, coned-shaped glass, cold but not iced. In the two short weeks they had been in Los Alamos together, this late afternoon cocktail moment had become a ritual. Everyone told him he had to eat something to go with it, that he was killing his brain cells and poisoning his liver, but this routine had become as diurnal an event as waking and sleeping. If any light in the building was on at midnight, it was most likely his.

"Do you want to read Ulam's letter?" he asked, after his first sip. "Knowing, now, that he's not in Sweden, tell me what this is all about."

She took the bait. "Of course it's not from him — but who ever played chess with you who would know you would be interested in this short game?"

"I did — I played chess with him — he came out to Berkeley looking for a job."

"Who else would have known that?"

"Linus Pauling. He was very dismissive of chess. He said he liked real problems, not man-made problems. And he was there at that Spring break when Ulam had a job interview. There was a lot of mathematics finally coming to bear in chemistry. That's what Pauling kept saying — 'these young guys, all they want to do is solve the Schroedinger equation — they don't want to build models — they don't want to get their hands dirty.'"

"But Pauling wouldn't write that kind of letter —"

"Of course not —"

"He would have said something to somebody else, though —"

"And bring in a chess game?"

"Sure — as an anecdote. He would have thought it peculiar...."

Oppie raised his glass in a toast. "Jonesy, did you ever wonder why I asked you to come out here, to this!" He swept his martini glass in a 180 degree arc.

"You liked my ass," she deadpanned.

"The way you bent over at the filing cabinets in Groves's office. In your Amelia Earhart trousers."

"Yeah, Earhart. Maybe she was a lez, but she had a slit in her ass."

"And you?"

"I'd jump in bed with you in a minute, but I won't be the 'other woman.' I happen to like what we're doing. Get it? What you and I are doing. And as far as sex goes, I just want to rub it in everybody's nose around here. Of course they think we're in the sack every night. Even though I sleep in the women's dorm. That's what I like about irrationality: people believe you can be in two places at once."

Oppie walked to his desk and pulled out a ruled pad. "I'll tell you why I wanted you out here." He wrote Atlantis, Utopia, Erewon, and Shangri-La on the sheet. "Look at them — all the ideal locations in the world. And now let's add this place to the list. Do you think we can do it? All the other made-to-order joints were based on some kind of spiritual isolation. This one's based on a simple thing — a science project."

"So whadaya call it? A commune? A paradise? A city on the hill?"

"A joint. Immune to the outside world. But still a joint where people who like the same thing come to share their work."

Kali Jones finished her martini and went to the sideboard to fix another. Oppie always started slowly, as if to delay the rush of that first sip that sent depth charges to the pit of the stomach. He watched her in a bemused way. She had a tomboy-like gait, like Barbara Stanwyck trying to tap dance. Kali was hardly the nurturing woman who ran the best hotel in town. She was all business, until she wasn't. Then she could soar over this room, any room.

"Do you think Los Alamos can join that list?" he asked her point blank.

"No," she answered with a smile. "It's the only one that's real."

And there it was: a rebuilt village on a hillside in the high country of New Mexico. For three weeks the Army trucks had discreetly plied their way along Route 66 from Dallas on the East to Tucumcari, and Los Angeles on the West to Gallup, then meeting at Albuquerque, then on up to Santa Fe, to deliver stoves and refrigerators, bunk beds and single beds and double beds, mess kits and silverware and porcelain, heaters and air-conditioners, pillows and blankets and sheets and towels, desks and blackboards, filing cabinets and foot lockers and dressers, soft drinks and hard liquor and wine and beer, provisions for a butcher shop, refrigerated shed for produce, ovens for baking, a bus doubling as a drugstore and a railroad car doubling as a hardware store. A glorified camp had been laid out on paper to fit into a town with just enough deserted homes and buildings to suddenly open their doors to habitation. What could not be requisitioned the Army Corps of Engineers could erect. It was, indeed, real.

"Can I tell you now, only now, why I really asked you to come here?"

"Finish your martini!"

"I'll tell you. I saw a person like my mother in you...."

"Oh Gawd!"

"My father was very successful in business. We came to New York from Germany before the War. The first, I mean. We had some money. We bought up on Riverside Drive when it was still cow country. He was in the rag business. His company made uniforms for the doughboys. Then suits for the gangsters. Good business, I'm told. But then my older brother and I saw what was really going on — before they shipped us out here for the summers. My mother kept the books. She put all the money into real estate. Not a penny in stocks. She remembered what inflation was like in the old country."

"What're you trying to tell me? That I'm a good manager like your mother?"

"Only better. If I learned anything in academia, it's that the professors know nothing except what they dream about. Their secretaries know how to run the university."

"Thanks. For all the secretaries of the world…."

"So yeah, Jonesy — I liked you at first sight. Now let's figure out what that letter means."

Kali Jones went to the desk and picked up the flimsy envelope. "First, I'd say it was intentionally brief. So it would slip through as just a whim, or if anybody bothered studying it they would just shrug. There's no return address. Just like an itinerant chessplayer. But you say this guy's a big mathematician?"

"Ulam is the kind of guy you want on your side. Sees things around the corner. Not afraid to speculate."

"So we've nailed down that somebody like Linus Pauling, who knew the value of Ulam, made this point to Lise Meitner."

"Yeah. But why didn't Pauling, or whoever it was, just write directly to you?"

"Ah! Meitner is the only one who can gauge how desperate the situation is. She — only she — could have originated that letter. Jonesy, this is a woman, trapped in Stockholm, who knows what the Germans are up to. She's a Jew. She knows what's happening to the Jews in Germany and now France. She's tired of writing to Einstein or Compton. So she makes up this fantastic idea of a letter from Ulam in Sweden. She knows we can find out quickly it's fake.

But — and get this — she also knows why we need a guy like Ulam."

"But the question remains, Sherlocke, where did she learn anything at all about Ulam?"

"Get on the train tomorrow to Boston. He's somewhere in Cambridge. Tell him I want him here in Utopia."

NINETEEN

February 22, 1942, The Reich Chancellery, Berlin

Adolph Hitler arrived punctually at eight in the morning at his spacious marble desk in the main hall of the ornate and imposing neo-gothic statehouse. The week's reports were due, and the news from the Russian front was hardly encouraging. His own motto — "Leningrad first, Moscow second" — had stumbled on both counts. Despite efforts of Finland's northern forces and Jodl's hand-picked Werhmacht generals, the city on the North Sea could not be completely surrounded and the starving populace refused to surrender. The graveyard of Napoleon's ambitions — Moscow — was equally resistant. Ice followed by snow and then mud left the German panzers mired in the outskirts of the Russian capital.

A stack of reports rested neatly in front of him. He banged a bell at his right and an orderly marched in. "Heil Hitler!" he chanted on cue. He knew enough not ask if the Fuehrer wanted coffee.

"Get Jodl. And Speer. Himmler, this morning. And let's get Goering out of the way first. Ja?"

Herman Goering knew he was the dog that needed kicking this time. The Battle of Britain was over, and the Luftwaffe hadn't prevailed. London was still burning, but there would be no fighting on the beaches, as Churchill agonized about. Hitler rose from his chair as the Air Marshall approached in tepid steps across the polished marble floor.

"Herman!" he said jovially. "It's time to think on a larger scale."

"I have the commanders' reports from the Eastern Front…"

"No, no! Put that aside. I want to know what you are doing with a certain Werner Von Braun. Eh?"

"Von Braun?"

"Yes. At Peenemunde. You know what I'm talking about—"

"You mean the rocket base—"

"Rockets, jet propulsion — it's all the same, isn't it?" Hitler settled into his chair again, allowing his large-framed cohort to sit as well.

"Very promising. Yes, now I remember. I have seen some films of actual manned aircraft over the North Sea."

"And Messershmitt is working on it, right?"

"Willy has designed a fighter without a gasoline engine. All rocket. Unfortunately…."

"Yes, I know. The first pilot was killed. A woman…. Have you issued a medal? "

"Lida Wassermann. Iron Cross."

"Good. But now I want to take a giant step above this. That's the trouble with these designers. Their idea of progress is baby steps. How about Heinkel, or Junker, or Focke-Wulf? Are they doing anything new?"

"Adolph — you know me. We fought together. I'm pushing these guys as fast as I can. What they need is a big kick in the rear end from you. You! You are the guy they fear."

Hitler opened the report on the top of the stack and spread it across the desk. "Look at this, here's Albert Speer. He built this place in a year, and it's bigger than anything in Paris or London. Right? No! It's also better than anything over there. That's what we need. Look what he's asking for now." He slid a sheaf of papers across the desk.

"Amerika Bomb?"

"That's right. He wants a plane that can deliver a bomb to New York. He drew this as soon as he heard about von Braun's rockets. This is no big fat balloon, like the Hindenberg. That baby almost bombed New York."

"I still think somebody over there hit it with a rifle."

"Just think about it — a bomb that could hit the Jews where they live." Hitler tapped the desk nervously, then rang the buzzer again. He nodded to the aide that gave the Heil Hitler salute. "Bring them all in. I want them all to hear this. Himmler, Doenitz, who else? Oh yes, Goebbels."

Goering rose to greet the new guests. His bulk more than his height towered over them all. He smiled broadly in the knowledge that he had been given a private conversation before they came in as a group. "The Fuehrer has a new idea," he ventured. "Not bigger. Better!"

The three newcomers took their seats, and squirmed. The propaganda chief, Goebbels, winced. Here we go again, he thought — what's it this time? They waited for the unveiling.

"Hermann is right. I just read the reports from Leningrad. And Moscow. We're being strangled. Just as we were in 1918. Not by the enemy. We're being throttled by the Jews!"

"Where?" Himmler asked. "We've got them in camps. Even our new friends, the French who ran to the south of France, have sent us trainloads of them. I mean trainloads."

"You don't remember! In 1918 the Jews were sitting in their banks and in their stores. They were making filthy lucre by making uniforms. They were gobbling up real estate by gobbling up profits from chemicals." Hitler kicked his chair back and began pacing back and forth behind his desk. "I was down there in the trenches. In the mud. In the filth of rotting flesh. Hermann — ah, Hermann! — he was up there in the clouds, in his Fokker…."

Goering closed his eyes. "The bullets killed you in the air as easily as on the ground."

"And where was Churchill when I was in the trenches? Where was Roosevelt? They were sitting on their fat behinds with their Jewish bankers fanning them with stocks!"

"So what's this have to do with Leningrad and Moscow?"

"This!" Hitler said, pounding the desk. "Wherever they are, the Jews control the money. And we can't win a war against armies that are building and building against us because they — they — have the money. It's that simple."

Admiral Doenitz knew how dangerous it was to speak without being called on. He had learned that in the previous war. But now he felt an overwhelming sense that he had something to say. "Herr Hitler, the Navy has good news. We are winning against the convoys. We are sinking their ships faster than they can build them."

"Yes?"

"We are picking them off along the Eastern coast of the United States, even before they join the convoy. My report is there on the table. But I'll say it now. They don't realize they are in this war. The Americans—"

"The Jews! I read your report, Admiral. Broadway in New York is lit up night after night like a Christmas tree. The Jews own Broadway. Do you think they'll shut it down? For a war across the world?'

"—And we can see the ships in our periscopes outlined against those lights. One torpedo and down they go. Down, down, down. They never know where the shots came from. Because they never turn off the lights!"

"But stop." Hitler again began to roam the room. The silence was ominous. Then he erupted again. "Get Leni Riefenstahl here. Yes, I said Riefenstahl. Joseph will know why...."

Goebbels looked at his cohorts with a wan smile.

"While we're waiting," Hitler continued, "May I tell you what Hermann was trying to tell you? You see, we were talking — before you joined us — about the difference between a baby step and a big step. In the war, you remember our great engineers had a cannon they called 'Big Bertha.' Joseph, what kind of a stupid name is that? It has the image of a hausfrau bringing a stuffed pig from the oven. They could barely get it on a railroad car — I think they had to make a new kind of railroad car. But this gun could hurl a ton of steel twenty miles or more. I don't remember. We buried our heads in the trenches and thought, maybe this thing will hit Paris and the French will give up and we'll all go home with our arms and legs with us. But it was a big dud! Yes, it set all those records. But it was just another bad joke — on us. So now what I'm trying to tell you is we're not going to win this

war by building a bigger gun. It's got to be a different gun —
beyond anything you can imagine. It's got to go through the
air with rocket power, not with propellers. And it's got to be
better than any kind of TNT ever invented. Can I tell you
what it is?"

Heinrich Himmler wanted to say, Shoot! But he kept his
tongue in check. Joseph Goebbels was still worrying about
what the film maker, Riefenstahl, had to do with this. Doenitz
and Goering felt they should have known, but like schoolboys
who failed to read the assigned chapter they were frozen in
their seats. This had better be a lulu, they all thought.

"No suggestions? Good! Does anybody know the name
Heisenberg? No? Or Strassman, or Hahn? Fair enough. This
isn't a science class. Gentlemen, these are people who are on
the road to getting us a super bomb, a bomb not like anything
anybody has ever seen before. There's a Jew you might have
heard of that gave us the idea. Yes, a Jew. A man named
Einstein. Himmler, you explain it. You're the guy if Speer's
not around. Or Speer...."

The man charged with "relocating" Jews from Germany
and Austria did indeed know something about physics.
Himmler had the pleasant duty of going through the lists of
all professors and graduate students at Kaiser Wilhelm
Institute, and he remembered all too well when Einstein left
Berlin in the early 'thirties. The wood and the fire that burns
the wood are part of the same thing, is the way he
remembered it. When all that's left is ashes, there's still heat
in the fireplace. Something as solid as wood has become
something as different as hot air. But the way it was explained
to him in his college physics classes, Einstein claimed that this
kind of thing happens all the time. And when it happens to
the basic elements, like iron or oxygen, things change from
something hard, something real, to something that's here and
then gone: heat or light or... energy! Thus the simple
equation: Energy equals Mass times a "constant" squared.
The 'constant' is just a polite word for some kind of regular

figure, which doesn't change with the types of materials involved.

Himmler said it as best he could: "We don't ordinarily go around talking about 'mass' or 'energy' — unless we're in the world of body-mass and how we feel when we're out of energy after a day's hard work." He could sense his cohorts were lost with even this simple example. So he changed course. "There's two things in the real world: mass and energy. One can become the other. When they DO change like that, sometimes there's a leftover. That leftover, gentlemen, is atomic power."

"OK. And what have our German scientists done about it?" Hitler asked, like a third-grade teacher facing a class of dunces.

"They found that a heavy element, like uranium, can easily break down, and change into something else. And when that happens there's always a leftover. The leftover is a whole lot of energy. That's the bomb, if you want to use it as a bomb. Since it comes from atoms changing from one form into another, it's called atomic energy." Speer was relieved that Himmler had delivered the dumbing down of atomic theory.

"Our job is to capture the results of that change, find a way to put it into a bomb, invent a way to ignite it. Maybe we should test it out at Leningrad...." Hitler banged the intercom once more. "Where's Riefenstahl? Where — is — she?"

Goebbels rose to the occasion. "London is still smoldering and no aircraft have ever appeared over Berlin. Do the people know this?"

"Just my point. What are we doing to shout this from the rooftops?"

"Pardon me, Joseph, but you changed the subject. What's this atomic science have to do with the war?"

Hitler walked to the wall and snapped on a switch that rolled down a world map. "Herr Goering, you are right. Let's get back to the war." He stabbed at the middle of North Africa. "General Rommel is showing how a war can be won.

He's driving the British back to the Suez Canal. With just a handful of Panzer tanks. He is so fast they think he's five times larger. When he reaches Suez, we will own the Middle East."

"Bravo!" Himmler blurted out.

"Now look at the Pacific. The Japanese came through and hit the battleships at Pearl Harbor. But did they follow through? They never do! Never!"

Doenitz knew it was his time to chime in. "If you're going to shoot the king, you've got to kill him. Isn't that Shakespeare? They had to invade Pearl Harbor. Or at least burn all their oil supplies. Now they've got a tiger by the tail..."

"Our U-boats have proved that. They're strangling the English." Hitler turned back to the map, and swept his hand across the United States. "But — and I'm sorry to say this — they can't strangle the Americans. They will wait us out! They will wear us down! They will do what they did in 1918. And then, you know what will happen, they will humiliate us again. They will confine us to a hog pen. They will take away our oil and our iron. They will make us beg for bread...."

"Adolph, Adolph!" Goering said. "Everything is going so well —"

"Can't you see ahead! We need...we need nothing less than the secret weapon. And we have it, right at our fingertips!"

The room snapped into silence. Himmler had just given the classroom lesson in physics. He knew what to say. "The bomb."

"And who is in charge of the bomb? Eh?"

"Heisenberg."

"When was the last time you had a report from Herr Heisenberg?"

Himmler squirmed in his chair. "He doesn't report to me...."

"Who does he report to?! Anybody? Jodl? Von Runstedt? And who does Von Braun report to?"

A bell rang and a voice on the intercom announced, "Frau Leni Riefennstahl is here."

A tall woman with flaxen hair and the grace of a ballerina swept in across the room. Men no longer raised eyebrows at her jaunty fashions of flowing blouses and slacks, for she was the Marlene Dietrich of German movie magazines. She favored a thin smile that highlighted her tanned and patrician face. Athletic and completely composed, she had the ageless beauty of a forty-year-old and one who preferred it to the naivete of a woman ten years younger. She thought briefly about giving the Fuehrer a kiss, just to disturb his guests, but then saw the seriousness clouding his face. "Sorry I'm slow getting here, gentlemen. I was out on a shoot."

Always the same answer, Hitler thought. What a profession! "Thank you, Frau Riefenstahl, for joining us. We have some serious business to discuss, and it involves you and Herr Goebbels, to begin with. Please, sit down. Now then, we've been talking about a gigantic project. Do you agree, gentlemen, that we need it to win the war?"

Goering had no inhibitions about disagreeing with his former comrade-in-arms. "But I thought you just showed how we are winning on all fronts. In London, in Paris, in Egypt…"

"In Moscow? In Washington? Didn't you hear me?! Give them enough time, and they will wear us down! We need the bomb." Hitler slumped in his chair as if to give up, then stalked again to the map, waving across the Pacific. "The Japanese thought they would make the Americans sue for peace. So they captured Wake Island, instead of Hawaii."

"Interesting you would mention Wake Island," Riefenstahl said. "I just saw their propaganda movie about it."

"What! The Japs captured it before Christmas. This is, what, less than two months ago…."

"The Americans move fast. They showed a preview at the Film Festival in Stockholm."

"You were there?"

"I just got back. A sob story. They massacre the invaders. Then they die at their gun mounts. Hollywood got the message. We've got to stamp out these runts with bad teeth and leering eyes, before they rape our nurses and our mothers."

Hitler appeared lost. "Stockholm? A film festival?"

"Sweden's a free country. Anyone can go in and out...."

Hitler pointed at Himmler. "Can what's her name, you know, the nuclear scientist, go in and out of Stockholm?"

"We've got more agents in Stockholm than there are banks in Switzerland. You mean Lise Meitner? She can't blow her nose without one of our guys offering a napkin."

"So you read all her mail?"

"Hahn and Strassman are on the team. They just give us her mail."

"Then what the hell's the roadblock? It's three years since they had this big idea. Do you understand? Three years!"

Himmler saw his opening: "In basic science, three years is not very long."

Hitler shot up and began pacing around the room. He stood still, finally, at a distance of forty feet, near the door where Riefenstahl had just entered. "Gentlemen," he shouted, "this conference is over. I'm tired of these asinine answers. 'In basic science'! What bullshit! Leni — you stay."

Leni Riefenstahl had long been rumored as having a serious romance with Hitler. His choice of Eva Braun ended that. But she had continued to idolize him. Her films of the Munich demonstration for the Nazi Party, in 1934, and for the Berlin Olympics, in 1936 , were world-renowned. Their names alone spoke of big ideas: The Triumph of the Will, and Olympia. Nothing small change about these titles. And she continued to hold out for something big, either in films or in politics. It didn't hurt to have the Fuehrer's ear. So she suspected her tete-a-tete with the leader would lead to something.

"Leni, you know Goebbels. You know what a ham-fisted bureaucrat he is. You are subtle. You get the big idea."

"Adolph, what are you trying to say? Of course I know the Gobbler."

"I want another great film. You say the Americans don't get it...."

"Right. All scare. All John Wayne. They only know Westerns."

"So what do you think of the Russians. Are they beating us? The image, I mean."

"Alexander Nevsky is a masterpiece. They make the German invaders out to be aristocratic knights on big horses, who throw children into bonfires. Of course, they have a pretty good soundtrack. Who is it? Prokoviev?"

"Are they seeing it in America?"

"In art houses. No big distributor will handle it. So, yes, it's not changing anybody's mind. What I try to do is change people's minds."

Hitler managed a broad smile. "And you did it! You showed the Negroes winning the races in Berlin. You showed that guy who could jump like a kangaroo..."

"Jesse Owens..."

"Yes! And you showed me scowling on the reviewers' stand! You made me human!"

"You were disappointed. That was the truth."

"That's what I want you to do — now. I want another Olympia! They all say were racists. Yes, we believe we are the master race. We think the Jews are not worthy of living with us. But what do the Americans think? They think THEY are the master race. They think the Negroes are not worthy of living with them. All these beautiful bodies from Africa — did they go back to America and take their place in society? I saw them hanging from trees, in nooses. I want you to get that in the film. Can you capture this? Can you?"

Riefenstahl raced Goebbels through her mind. Yes, she could do that. She ran Hollywood through her mind. Yes, all the studios she knew there could make such a film. She knew what Hitler wanted, and what he wanted her to tell him. But she knew it was wrong. It was too late for long-term propaganda. It was too late for something that would change the image of a rapacious invader to that of a trapped survivor. But how to break it to him?

At length she twirled her hair impatiently, as if unable to solve the problem. Then she went to the map. "The newsreels and the news people dominated the film festival in Stockholm," she said. "Everything is guns and bombs and people fleeing cities in carts with all the belongs they have. It's a barrage of evil, no matter who has caused it. Can we overcome that barrage? Adolph, this is not our secret weapon."

"Then what is?"

"You tell me. I heard talk of a bomb. Do you have a name for it? This is all I know — names and images. You and I, let's name it."

"Something simple, like 'Olympia'?"

"Yes, very classical. That one was perfect. The mountain in Greece that symbolizes the whole event. The classical touch. The purity of athletics — when even we, the ones who were controlling the performance, showed our Aryan athletes coming in second to men from Africa. So we sent the message that we are fair. We believe we are the best, but when we are bested, we accept it!"

Hitler waited patiently, but his ardor had cooled. "Do you need more time? Do you want to think about it and phone it to me?"

"No," she said softly. "It's obvious. Something that captures all the devastation and misery and blood all over the place. Lots of blood. And combine it with mystery. Then it just may accomplish...."

Hitler looked at her quizzically. "So what is your name for it?"

She closed her eyes and tried to put together two things: secrecy and blood. Then she said, at last, "Code Red."

TWENTY

February 23, 1942, The White House, Washington, D.C.

Henry Stimson brought an international perspective to his job as Secretary of War. Born just after the end of the Civil War, he moved in all the right circles of his Patrician upbringing, his Republican associations, and his Wall Street connections, through financial turmoil as well as political upheavals, but he was never a partisan. When Roosevelt asked him, in the gathering storm of Hitler's rise to power, to join his cabinet, he saw nothing untoward about serving in a left-leaning administration. This was war on the horizon, and the country had to use its best resources to fight it. The first thing he needed to do, he realized after surveying the Army and Navy he had to run, was to find out what was going on in the rest of the world.

"Get me Wild Bill Donovan," he told the President after settling into his office. "I can't run this place on hunches."

"Frank Knox told me the same thing yesterday. Two out of two is pretty good." Roosevelt smiled his broadest smile, because he knew that Stimson was well aware of Roosevelt's friendship with Colonel Donovan — going back to their college days at Columbia.

"Have you seen his reports on Hitler. And on Churchill?"

"He hand-delivered 'em."

"So he'll take the job?"

"He even has the name picked. Office of Special Services. How discreet. He loathes the FBI. And Hoover loathes him. He loathes the argument about who should run the war in the Pacific. And Mac Arthur loathes him."

"So it's OSS? Good. But how do we get a hold of Donovan? Is he still at that law firm in Manhattan?"

"Henry, I'm way ahead of you. I told him five months ago to pick himself an office, near his place in New York. We cleared all the deadwood out of the Army and Navy spooks. He's at Room 3603, Rockefeller Center. Want his phone number?"

"Franklin, you devil! So he's going to work out of New York."

"Exactly. The Navy's moving things all over the place to get the Pentagon in place. Much too slow. Let the Navy go to New York if they have to see him."

"And what are you and I going to do — go to New York?"

"Bill loves the water. I'll have him come down to the Potomac."

When Roosevelt called Bill Donovan that evening, he asked him to give a report on the mind-set of Adolph Hitler to a select group aboard the Potomac the next day. He thought some of Stimson's staff would especially be impressed. Stimson made a point of telling the President how insular the bureaucrats were. "They build impressions of people based on stories in the press. They glorify people. They denigrate people. Mussolini is a buffoon. Franco is a genius." His word of advice to Roosevelt was to resist any judgment until meeting face to face. And having a drink with him.

There was a chill on the Potomac as Roosevelt's guests came aboard that wintry evening. Washington always hoped to pick up harbingers of Spring by that time, but it was not to be. The President himself was wrapped in a blanket as he welcomed his friends aboard from his deck chair, cigarette holder perched upward in his lips, tumbler of scotch in his right hand. When Donovan lurched up the gangplank, somewhat late, he was greeted by Stimson, Knox, and a young woman carrying an attache case and a notebook. As the three of them went into the ship's cabin, Donovan stood, somewhat in awe, before the President. At 59, he was feeling his age, despite his rugged features and trim condition. His friends always kidded him about his resemblance to Pat O'Brien, the film star who seemed always to play the roles of police captains or Catholic priests. But Donovan would have none of the stereotype. He was a fighter.

"First, I assume you'll have a drink," Roosevelt said. "Tell me what you're doing. Then let the guys ask the questions inside. What'll it be?"

"Got any decent beer, Mister President?" The one thing Donovan knew from long experience was to be the last one in any meeting to have one too many. A breeze was already shimmering on the water. He held out his hand.

"At last I've met someone from the Fighting Sixty-Ninth," Roosevelt intoned. Despite his Fireside chats, his self-proclaimed interest in the 'common man,' he knew very well that he had trouble with the give and take of ordinary conversation. He felt it since his days as Secretary of the Navy in the first war. He could never shake the vernacular of the government official, the politician, the orator. Eleanor had tried for all their mismatched marriage to dissolve that patrician tone, that ring of history in the humblest thought. Lucy Mercer didn't bother to try.

"At last I've met a president," Donovan answered without missing a beat. "Let's go inside — you didn't have to wait for me on deck...."

Roosevelt continued talking as he pushed his wheelchair toward the cabin door. "Tell me something. Is it really true about the songs the sixty-ninth sang as they walked up to the front?"

"Oh — that...."

"....That you sang 'Give My Regards to Broadway" as you passed your buddies coming out?"

"Yeah. We violated the silence rule. That wasn't the only rule we violated. Sometimes rules are meant to be violated."

As the cabin door swung open, Stimson and Knox rose respectively. The young woman, who had removed her coat and was busily fixing drinks, cast a quick glance at Donovan. Her eyes lit up in recognition. "Dad! So they finally got you down here!"

"Are you sure you want this job?" Donovan rasped.

"So we get two for the price of one," Roosevelt deadpanned. "Or I guess I should say, so we all know each other, right?"

"Nepotism," Donovan agreed.

———————

As was his custom, Stimson set the agenda for the meeting in a few unvarnished sentences. "Mr. Donovan, this is all about you and your new organization. The President rightly saw that we needed a focused intelligence effort. Call it the OSS or whatever you want, it's our spy program. And we have one overriding goal — to find out what the Germans are doing to create an atomic weapon and to make sure we can prevent them from doing so. Do we agree?"

Kelly Donovan began scribbling at a furious pace as Knox was the first to reply. "More important than knowing where the Japs will strike next?" he said without a trace of contentiousness.

"Yes," Stimson answered. "We've broken their code, up to a point, and it'll only get better. The black room in Honolulu is miraculous. Nimitz tells me they're following their game plan, and he's ready to box with 'em."

"But how real is this atomic bomb talk?" Knox persisted.

"Donovan, you probably know more than anybody here," Stimson cut in. "The floor is yours."

Donovan glanced quickly at Roosevelt. "I'll need more than a few minutes, Mr. President," he said, "but the short answer is we're in real trouble. May I back up a bit?"

"You may back up to the creation, Mister Donovan. We're here to listen. And to you."

Donovan had always felt better talking on his feet. Perhaps it was from his brief stint as a trial attorney. He rose and stood back from his audience. "Thanks," he began with a nod to the President. "I'm glad you mentioned the Fighting Sixty Ninth. What was that? Twenty-five years ago? When I met Hitler at the 1936 Olympics in Berlin, he tried to pull that 'Where were you in the war?' pitch on me. I told him I was in the trenches. For all I know, we were across the same bloody, muddy no-man's-land. See, I was part of the American Olympic delegation, so he thought I was a former boxer or something. So I asked him if he was a fight fan. The interpreter took a while to get that right, but then Hitler's eyes lit up. Oh, we have the world champion, Max Schmeling, he said. And I told him we have the real champion, Joe Louis. So we went back and forth on that one. Then we got into the Jews...."

Donovan could sense Stimson and Knox wondering where all this was going. So he took his time, went to the bar and picked up a beer, and waited to see if they were still simmering. He knew instinctively that he had Roosevelt's full attention.

"I knew at that moment," Donovan said," that this guy doesn't talk through his hat. And the point is this, Hitler has followed through on everything he told me about the Jews. And he's going to follow through on everything he's saying about the bomb."

"Wait a minute," Stimson interrupted. "What has Hitler said about any kind of a bomb?"

"Just my point. That's what we're picking up."

"From where?" Knox asked skeptically.

"Slow down for a minute and I'll elaborate. We have three guys at Los Alamos, and it's not even up and running yet. We have a guy in Czechoslvakia, at the uranium mines. We have three guys at M1 in London. We have a guy following Werner Heisenberg all around Europe, not a small feat. And we have a guy in Stockholm, which may be our best resource."

Stimson pursued Knox's line of skepticism. "What exactly is the German plan? Do we really have something hard?"

"How does this sound?" Donovan asked. "Heisenberg is the leader of a group called the Uranium Club. Not your usual German strip joint. It's part of Ordnance in the Reich Research Council. Sounds like bureaucracy, but we're familiar with that. They have a three-year lead on us. Three years! Hitler always bragged to me about how the Americans all came to Germany in the 'twenties to get their tickets punched. Then they went back to being professors at Cal Tech and Columbia and UC. But the Germans stayed there, except maybe for Einstein and other Jews who went to England. So that three-year lead is very troubling. I tell you we're facing a disaster...."

Roosevelt waved his hand as he lit another cigarette. " Mister Donovan, your report is very distressing. Do you have the manpower to keep on this?"

"We can always use more. As long as you write the checks, we'll be OK. But remember, I'm only the messenger. It's you guys that have to take action when we have to throw a monkey wrench into the Germans' front yard."

"Are you having trouble?" Roosevelt asked.

"I may need help with the Navy," Donovan answered mysteriosuly.

"But Churchill told me his aircraft had disabled the German bomb program by blasting some dams in Norway."

"Great story," Donovan laughed. "The German scientists went down the wrong road, and then the Brits went out and blasted the wrong road."

"Wait a second. You mean those 'dam busters' were phony?" Stimson asked painfully.

"Not phony. British intelligence found that the Germans were bringing heavy water in from Norway. Heavy water is just water with a higher concentration of hydrogen in the water. So the Brits assumed the Germans were on to something. As it turned out, the whole deal is uranium. That simple."

"What's this about Czechslovakia?" Knox broke in.

"Big uranium mines there. But you know something? This time the Germans really blew it."

Roosevelt nodded and raised his glass. "I'm liking this story better and better. Could Hemingway make this up?"

"No, he couldn't. Here comes a guy out of left field, our man, Robert Oppenheimer, and he goes to Czechslovakia and convinces them to ship all their uranium stores to the U.S. This is just before December 7th. And you know what? They do it!"

"Where, for God's sake, did they ship it?" Knox asked.

"To Manhattan. Yes, to a warehouse on the west side that you guys probably wouldn't want to go to in a million years. But there it is. Uranium, sitting in a place just above Hell's Kitchen."

Roosevelt had to chuckle. "I suppose I lost my touch. I should have named this the Hell's Kitchen Project."

"What did you name it?" Knox asked.

"It named itself, the President said with a broad grin. What else but The Manhattan Project?"

TWENTY-ONE

March 1, 1942, Richmond, California

Henry Kaiser was beside himself. He ripped another month off his desk calendar — admittedly, a short month — and tossed it into his waste basket. He didn't like losing bets. Especially when he wrote them on banners throughout the shipyard. "Two Liberties by March!" they proclaimed. Now he'd have to throw those in the waste basket, too.

The *Patrick Henry* was the first down the ways, just before the end of the year. It was his New Years' present to the President. In the water not quite three months from the initial design to the finished product, built by a yard that had never built a rowboat before. The papers laughed at it, of course. A big, tubbish 400 feet of welded steel, thick in the middle and heavy on top. And that was before it was outfitted with cranes and lifeboats and hatch covers and gun mounts and gun tubs. Yes, guns. Congress made haste, even before Pearl Harbor, to allow "armed guards" to operate the machine guns and cannons aboard merchant marine vessels. Now the idea of a cargo ship as a fighting ship was built into the design, even of a vessel as clumsy looking as a Liberty ship.

The first reports back from *Henry* were good. "I didn't choose the name," Henry Kaiser said. "But I'm still a proud father." The low center of gravity of the 'tub' tended to give it a whiplash effect up top. In the language of the trade, it had some "stiffness" that made it more susceptible to rolling. If ballast could be properly secured 'tween decks, that roll could be minimized. The use of wlding throughout, rather than rivets, contributed to a sense of rigidity. The *Patrick Henry* made its first trip to Bora Bora and back in just over a month, cargo delivered safely and a happy crew.

Kaiser was now convinced he could find ways to cut the construction time in half. Two, three, maybe four yards working at once. Most of all, doubling up on the welders. Maybe a Henry-Ford type answer: move the product through the work force — weld and prefab sections for two ships at once.

He liked to view the world through the lens of Life magazine. He was finishing up Grand Coulee Dam, in 1936, when he saw photographs of seamen burning in the oil around sinking ships in the Spanish Civil War. Water on fire. The current issue of Life had more death: Filipino soldiers being bayoneted by Japanese soldiers on the Bataan peninsula. He walked out of the new movie, "Wake Island," because it was make-believe. Henry Kaiser was a realist. He didn't take to propaganda.

He flipped through his daily reports quickly. There were no problems, but also no ideas for doing things differently. The financials didn't concern him at all. One of his best managers, his son, kept an eye on tardiness and sick-outs. At the top of the report, his son scribbled, "Maybe we need an incentive better than pay? Awards?"

Incentives bothered Henry Kaiser, mainly because he had never needed one. He had been running full-steam since he was a teenager selling newspapers. His incentive was doing something nobody else could do. But how to make other people feel the same way he did? He didn't know.

He checked his watch and was surprised to find, as he usually did at that time of the day, the morning had vanished in a blizzard of paperwork. He walked through the mess hall and picked a table where five women and a man were finishing their sandwiches. "Can I join you for a minute?" he asked. "What's good?"

"Hamburgers."

"Sold."

They knew 'the boss' well enough to take him at face value. He was everywhere, he was nowhere. There was no corporate dining room at the yard. One thing he never did:

ask about 'the children at home.' Husbands, wives, kids, personal problems — off limits. Gripes, ideas, little suggestions, complaints — fair game.

Maria O'Hara chose to violate the rule today. It just came straight out of her mouth, unbidden, unplanned, unformed "My son is now stationed at Treasure Island," she said. "He's going to be assigned to the next ship down the line. That is, whenever we finish it."

Ah, Kaiser thought — just what I needed, another reason to worry about how fast we can get the next Liberty down the ways. The hamburger was giving him heartburn, but he champed down hard. He held his napkin to his lips to give himself time to reply. "What's he doing at Treasure Island?"

"Gunnery, he tells me. But he's assigned to the engine room, so I don't know how much shootin' he's gonna be doin.'"

"He's in the Navy?"

"No, merchant marine. They're getting ready to man the ship, he tells me. They have to learn everything that everybody else does on the ship. So I guess that's where gunnery comes in."

"Do you mind if I ask you your name?"

"O'Hara. His is Edwin Joseph. Edwin Joseph O'Hara. He'll be nineteen soon. I want this next ship you make to be the damnedest finest ship you can make, Mister Kaiser."

The other women at the table didn't know what "got into" their friend. Maria was always the quiet one. She didn't know, herself, what "got into" her. She turned away, embarrassed. The silence was thick. One of the women got up, and without excusing herself, walked away. Kaiser wasn't sure what he saw, but she seemed to him to be stifling tears.

"Mrs. O'Hara," he said, with a slight catch in his voice, "I have a son. I think I know what you mean. I hope I know what you mean. I'll do my best." He stood somewhat awkwardly and looked hopefully in the eyes of the others at the table. Had he said the right thing? Was he any good at all at this sort of thing? Did he have a moral to impart — a pep talk to make? At last, he said what he realized was the only thing he could say, "I'll do my best."

"We know you will," the others around the table chimed in, awkwardly. The man in the group looked down at the table as he decided to add something, as if afraid to look anyone in the eye. "The woman who just left — she lost her only son just a couple of days ago. Down in San Diego. In the Navy."

"How did that happen?" Kaiser said softly.

"Airplane accident. He just got his stripes at Pensacola. Came out here. Ran into a buddy's propeller."

Henry J. Kaiser sat back down at the table. "What're we going to do for her?"

"He's gonna be buried at the cemetery in San Francisco — what do they call it? Colma, I think." Maria knew at lot more about the family, but she decided it was time to end the chit-chat. What did it matter that the three of them had gone up to the Top of the Mark in San Francisco for a glorious view and a glass of champagne? She was jealous of her friend, with an All-American son who had earned an officer's rank. That was then. Now she couldn't imagine what it must be like to lose a son like that. In the blink of an eye. For what?

"OK, back to work," the young man said, mostly to ease the tension.

But Maria decided she wasn't finished. "I learned something, just a little thing. I learned the name of a hotel in San Francisco. 'Cause Juliette and her son and I went up there for a drink at the Top of the Mark."

"Ah, the Mark Hopkins...." Kaiser said. "My wife and I have gone there a lot over the years."

"Yeah, so what I learned was the name Hopkins."

"Oh? Why is that something you wanted to learn?" Kaiser asked.

"See — it's the name of the ship we're workin' on. Your next baby. I can't wait to see it born." Maria waited for him to bite, but when he didn't, she announced triumphantly, "Hopkins. The Stephen Hopkins."

TWENTY-TWO

March 2, 1942, Stockholm, Sweden

George Townsend had studied horses as a hobby while attending Cal. Horse racing had its attraction for him, but mainly he liked to ride and to get to know the horse he was riding with. Not on, with. That was his attitude. He had learned a lot from horses, just by watching them. He noticed in particular that two horses in the wild usually sleep standing up, side by side, but looking in the opposite direction. Big eyes and all, they knew the value of 'watching your back.'

George felt the heat on his back the moment he left his compliant Nordic overnight girlfriend. He made his way to the ferryboat dock as fast as his legs could carry him, and he was in Copenhagen before he even had time to get off a radio message to Washington. This was definitely not the time to try to connect with Lise Meitner.

"Lay low for a while," the wire came back from D.C. He used the time to learn all he could about Niels Bohr, though he wasn't about to approach him in his home town. Nevertheless, he worked his way into enough conversations to convince himself that there was one overriding issue in developing an atomic bomb: the sheer quantity of uranium.

It kept coming back: forget "heavy water." That was an operational concern. Maybe the SS was on his back. Maybe the Gestapo. But as long as he played the role of the itinerant college student, just hanging around Bohr's Institute, he was out of the spotlight. This meant two things: first, the Germans had an intense interest in keeping Lise Meitner out of touch with the Unites States, and, second, this surely had something to do with her knowledge of uranium. Not just its chemical reactions, but where it could be found and why huge quantities were needed to make a bomb.

In a month of patient waiting, George Townsend had plenty of time to grow a fearsome beard and to shrink his weight from that of an out-of-practice rugby player to that of a platform diver. One month — that's all it took. It was a fateful month, from what he read in the Danish papers, in the world scene. The Japanese had the run of the Pacific, from the outer islands of Hawaii down to Australia. MacArthur had retreated down the Bataan peninsula to try to hold the line around the island fortress of Corregidor. Then, almost as quickly, Roosevelt ordered the General to evacuate himself and his command staff to Australia. With Japanese Zeroes controlling the skies against the feeble force of U.S. P-40s, it took an American submarine to complete the maneuver — and at night. Even in newsprint-hungry Denmark, a banner headline filled the papers: "I Shall Return."

While headlines in the United States focused on the Japanese rampage through the South Pacific, it was painfully evident throughout Holland, Denmark, and the Scandinavian countries that there was something more ominous at stake further toward China and Burma. Oil. The 'Japanese Sphere of Influence," so loudly proclaimed before the war as the goal of the Empire, was now achieved by force of arms. The oilfields of Southeast Asia were falling, month by month, to advancing Japanese forces.

The British led out briefly at Singapore, but soon Japanese admirals went straight to the prize: Indonesia. On the other side of the world, Hitler's panzer units raced into the oil fields of Rumania. Tojo's strike forces had accomplished even more. There was something eerie about reading all about this in a Danish newspaper, Townsend thought. Which way would the United States look — East or West?

Finally, on this brisk March day, George received the call he had been waiting for. It was a simple radio message, barely coded, well away from the U.S. embassy in Copenhagen. It was straight from Bill Donovan's office in Manhattan, as simple as an order for another shipment of Coca Cola for an upcoming football game. It read, in and among lines of gibberish:

Massage the lady. U can do. Go Bare!

No reply necessary, Townsend knew. Crude, just gauche enough to look like a college prank. But the meaning was clear. It was now do or die at the Institute. He glanced at the mornng paper as he again boarded the ferry for Stockholm, but this time emaciated, bearded, and disheveled. The headline read, "Hitler proclaims, "We shall begin our health only by eliminating the Jews."

"Eliminating?" Hadn't they already been shipped in cattle cars to concentration camps from Poland to rural Austria to just outside Munich? This was a change in plans? Was any doubt now that Hitler was going to employ what he had threatened. The Final Solution.

When I got myself into this, he told himself, I was warned I could easily be killed. A cyanide capsule was his only protection against excruciating torture. It fit neatly into his baggy wallet. Now it was crunch time. The Manne Sigbahn Institute, he repeated as if in a dream. How could he get in there without bringing a cordon of German agents in with him? Perhaps, he thought, perhaps a delivery job? No, too easy. Everyone here wore uniforms, identifying badges, caps, jackets, almost like football players with numbers on their jerseys.

The ferry ride was far too short, this time. He had run out of ideas. A beggar? No, beggars here were all too invisible. No stopping in a bar, this time. That's the first thing an American would do, and he had fallen into it like a fly into a pot of honey. He grabbed his bag, now slimmed down to the essentials, and waited his turn to disembark. No need to hurry. Think. Look around.

Then he saw her. It was a youngish woman, wearing a shawl, carrying a baby well wrapped against the early winds of the Spring air, just ahead of him on the gang plank. He could barely see a wisp of hair in the pouch the woman had formed with her baby's blanket. Could he...? Nah — men don't carry babies around. Besides, where would he commandeer a baby?

He walked through the station waiting room and searched for other ideas. Out of the corner of his eye he saw a bearded young man approach the woman with the baby, take the 'pouch' from her, and plant a welcoming kiss on her cheek. It was all so natural. She took his valise, stretched her arms as if to shake off the cramps of carrying a bundle on a long ferryboat ride. Then the two strode out of the terminal, hand in hand, with the bearded young man happily caressing the well-wrapped baby.

Or was it a baby? Who could tell? It was worth a try.

Avoiding the well-worn paths of the waterfront, Townsend headed toward the City Center with a new found purpose. Sure enough, he came upon a commercial street with small shops under two and three story apartment buildings. A used clothing store is what he wanted, but he found even better: a second-hand children's store. He hadn't expected to find a life-size doll, but there it was. One heavy blanket, one embroidered coverlet, and a cloth hat completed his new role.

In a small park just outside the store, Townsend made simple work of his bag and its minimal contents. His toiletries, such as they were, went into his heavy coat pockets. He filled out the bottom of his well-wrapped baby pouch with his radio equipment and notebooks. When he was finished with his make-shift disguise, that of a young father on the way home from a child care facility — what else? — he sat back for a few minutes and rehearsed his role. Yes, he told himself, it was a very young baby. He would support the head carefully in the back. He would hold 'her' high, just under his chin. Yes, but he had to move on, or come into someone's area of suspicion.

After a few blocks of brisk walking, without seeming to raise any eyebrows from passing bike riders and pedestrians, he searched in his pockets for his map of the city. Yes, the

Manne Sigbanne was not far from the city center. He would have to come up with a reason for entering, he expected, but he was wrong. It was near closing time, and the procession of people in and out was brisk enough for him to join in without any cause for alarm. Perhaps he had pulled it off. Perhaps the German agents that ringed the place thought him just another anxious father. He expected the worst — a tap on the shoulder, a jab in the ribs. But now he was inside. Maybe it was his faintly disreputable appearance, maybe it was his clutching of his 'baby' — perhaps the combination of the two....

When he found the room where Lise Meitner worked, he half expected her to be listed as 'on vacation' or 'at conference' or just not working today. But then he realized she was working as merely a lab assistant. He had looked at photographs of her for two months. He had listened to recordings of her voice at scientific conferences. Yet he had little idea of what he would see in this basement laboratory, or whether he would know her if he saw her.

But, at once, he did. She gave him a quizzical smile. Surely you have stumbled into the wrong room, her manner said. There was no one else in the room. He closed the door and set down his bundle. At once she laughed. "You must be an American," she said. "This is just too ridiculous." Then: "Don't worry. The place isn't bugged. I've made sure of that."

Over the next thirty minutes, George Townsend scribbled down the most important notes of his note-taking career. "The only thing you can't do from here," she told him, "is try to make radio contact. This building is all static, and for good reason. What you've just heard not even Hahn and Strassman, or even Heisenberg, understand. I can't get it out by mail — not any more. They have clamped down all over the place."

"Keep talking," he said.

"Get the hell out of here are get this information to Oppenheimer. The Germans now know they need tons of uranium ore. And the only place they can get the high grade they need is from the Congo."

"What? How do you know about Oppenheimer? He was appointed to the Manhattan Project just this month!"

"I just got back from Copenhagen myself. I had one long message there — from your boss. What's his name?"

Townsend especially enjoyed pronouncing his boss's full name after the charade he had gone through today. "His name is Donovan. Wild Bill Donovan."

TWENTY-THREE

March 17, 1942, Libreville, French Equatorial Africa

Four longboats sputtered into the cosseted harbor of the bay. A single long wooden pier urged them on, it seemed, as willing dock workers blinked to make out the specifics of their new visitors. The magistrate of the town, now under the mantle of Vichy France, had his orders: identified or not, vessels docking here were to be cleared through his office. That office contained a melancholy German officer, posted for just such an occasion. He hurried along the pier to join the magistrate and complete his reports.

The vessel anchored in the harbor wasn't flying flags, at least that he could see. It had a sleek appearance, with a prominent bow, not just a merchantman from the Channel, but a North Sea, ice-breaker type. He noted that the front works of the vessel, the forward cabin, was especially elongated. That seemed clumsy. But this was not ordinary ship. A large canvas tarp hung over the prow where the vessel's name would ordinarily be obvious.

Then another surprise appeared on the horizon — a ship even larger, perhaps 500 feet overall, but even more obviously heavy in beam. Before the motor boats from the first vessel docked, the German officer could see that this was a well-identified cargo ship. A swastika hung from its upper deck, and the name 'Tannefels' soon was obvious on its prow. The officer was suddenly thrown into the shock of the world war that had been distant for two years. Nothing in this remote under bellow of Africa for month after month, and now two visitors of massive proportions were on top of him. All of this without wires or news of any kind.

Fortunately, the French superintendent of this French 'protectorate' had a clear understanding of what the Vichy government wanted. They wanted to avoid being killed, in return for ignoring their conscience. As they had argued in the bars of the town ever since France had surrendered to the Nazis, what is this thing called 'conscience,' any way?

The German crews in the long boats went straight to their tasks, without as much as a salute or a request for water. They hauled flexible metal pads to the beaches beside the pier and created a crude but effective roadway for heavier equipment. Within an hour the *Tannenfels* had beached several large trucks onto the metal treadways, without incident. A scraggly assembly of workers, shopkeepers, and barmaids from the town's bars had gathered into an informal delegation along the beach to observe the half-tracks spin ashore and regroup on what was decorously known as 'First Street.' The German drivers viewed the crowd with amusement, mixed with lechery aimed at the occasional French fille displaying her *decolletage*.

Officers from *Tannerfels* soon also were ashore from speedboats, bringing both voracious noise and a sense of drama to a town long descended into languidness. As usual on an early Spring day, the sun beat down unchallenged by the merest breeze. The German officers in the long coats and stiff, tall dress hats soon felt out of place — but what could they do?

"We will not burden your beautiful city," the skipper from *Tannenfels* proclaimed to the town's only dignitary. "We must move inland quickly!" His truck drivers shrugged in another disappointment. Two weeks at sea without women, and now that we're here and they're here we're leaving for another two seeks in the bush!

In a matter of minutes, the truck convoy from Libreville left only diesel fumes and the sounds of whistles behind. The waves returned to their gentle rocking. The crews from the long boats rolled their mesh roadways into neat coils and packed them away. To their great chagrin, the crews were commanded to return to their mother ship. Four officers, one from each boat, accepted the invitation of the German 'consul,' as he wished to call himself, to "have a beer."

Of the three bars in the town, only one had a space for a musical performance — but such a space was very much part of the French tradition, no matter how small the village. The Vichy magistrate and his German cohort apologized that this small sign of culture was not indicative of the general countryside. "But you don't want to venture far from the town," they advised. "There are criminals everywhere, without a conscience."

A quick round of beers soon led to schnapps. "It's not necessary to return to the Spier tonight," one of the officers rationalized. "The captain told us to use our judgment, to make friends with the locals. This is a very sensitive assignment."

The magistrate nodded, filing away in his mind, as he did, the name "Spier." No great significance to this, he thought, but at least I now know *something*."

At a nearby table, a scraggly young man appeared to take pains to avoid contact with the foreign entourage. He was more interested in the two young Frenchwomen hanging on his every word. He quoted Verlaine to them, he quoted Proust. Then he reached back further into history and quoted Montaigne. His French was just adequate, but his backlog of quotations endless. Of course he had learned this at Cal: never underestimate the fascination of women for wit.

George Townsend thought for a minute about going straight to the gut with these German officers, but then he decided not to press his luck. He had been quite lucky to follow up on Lise Meitner's advice and get to the French Congo as soon as possible. He was lucky to find a monthly supply vessel that called at all the ports from Liberia to the Belgian Congo. He was luckiest of all to settle on Libreville as the logical destination for the German convoy.

And now he had substantial information. These were serious ships — even *Stier* had more than 400 men aboard. And that was just the 'protection' — a Q boat, with gun emplacements cleverly hidden behind a fake extra-long forward cabin. As much as he wanted to spend another night of revelry with the French barmaids, he decided to cut the evening short to get his messages across as soon as he could. The fond adieus were good for his ego, and raised an eyebrow with the German guests, who perhaps felt they deserved as much.

He knew the wireless operator at the local paper would still be at his desk. He scribbled a message and passed it to the operator. Vichy or not, he was French. He shook Townsend's hand before he sent:

Donovan: They are here for U. Would not be unless they know. God, man! George

TWENTY-FOUR

March 28, 1942, Rockefeller Center, New York City

Bill Donovan made his customary stop for coffee at Flanagan's Bar on East Forty-Ninth Street, within sight of the ice-skating rink just beyond on Fifth Avenue. It was perfect weather for skating. At 6:45 in the morning, it required a 'sweetener' in the java to take the chill off. Bartenders would not be on duty for another four hours, but the morning swamper knew what to do.

Donovan scanned the *Daily News*, caught in that no-man's-land between the end of football for the Giants and the prospect of Spring training for the Yankees. In a matter of thirty minutes he would have the most comprehensive briefing in the country on how the war was going—from Stalingrad to Corregidor. But he still counted on the journalists at the daily rag to have something for his eyes. Maybe a letter, maybe a scandal.

After two slugs of coffee-and, the best part of the day for him was the ride to the 37th floor. The elevator guys were either Jimmy Cagney tough guys or Fred Astaire dreamers. Each one of them knew he would make it, one day. Each one of them knew who came and when they came, when they parted their hair for lunch and when they tightened their ties for dinner. They recorded everything in their noggins and they knew when to rewind the tapes. Donovan liked to catch them off guard, maybe with a fancy menu under his arm or a bouquet of roses wrapped in the paper. It was the game he was in, and they were among the best players he could imagine.

He opened the door to his law office, turned on the lights, checked the recepionist's desk for any late-night deliveries, and went to the mailroom. As usual, there were two baskets waiting for him, one with 'official' mail and the other with the essentials, carefully winnowed by his long-time secretary, Stella, who always made sure that the 1 A.M. edition of the *New York Times*, with reviews of the previous evening's Broadway openings, was on top. He knew he wouldn't have time for the crossword today, a Friday, because there had to be a report, by one means or another, from George Townsend. Eleven days had gone by since his cryptic radio message from the Congo.

Donovan's eyes lit up. There it was, a large packet, postmarked Lisbon, Portugal. How in the hell did he get to Lisbon? Donovan wondered. No matter: one by one the envelopes inside said it all. There were photographs of German ships arriving at Libreville: *Stier* and *Tannenfels*. There was a map of the route of German truck convoys into the mountains. Then the coup: actual samples of ore from the mines. Townsend had even given instructions for metallurgical analysis: "Get this to Columbia for calibration and check with Oppenheimer." Finally, there was a two-page, carefully hand-written letter:

Donovan: I sure as hell hope this gets to you, fast. Yes, my wire says they're in the Congo for uranium. Big time. I counted forty trucks and a crew of maybe three hundred Nazi grunts. No SS hanging around. The Navy guys drink in the bars while the grunts are out bulldozing the hills. The French are no dummies — they knew this was coming. One guy in town has assay samples of everything from gold to diamonds. Who could tell uranium would be the deal? But the krauts must have taken samples on their own. They don't throw all that equipment and manpower around for easter eggs! I'm hanging in Lisbon until you tell me what to do. It's full of SS types, just like Stockholm. Orders, please! I check the U.S. consulate every day. Here are all the specs on the German ships:

Donovan didn't bother waiting for Stella to arrive: it was still only seven-thirty. He called Henry Stimson's private line in Washington with a simple message: "I'm on the 8 o'clock train to Washington. Urgent we talk and bring Navy people on board."

Donovan's cab to Penn Station left him ample time to bundle his mail onto the club car and call back to his office to confirm his whereabouts. As the Express lurched out of the station, he was already scribbling on a legal pad. This was the first test of what the OSS was all about. This was the time to show Roosevelt that he was right in creating a separate agency to handle the big-ticket items. This was the moment to demonstrate that this former foot soldier was the right man to jump into decisions that could win or lose the war.

But his heart wasn't racing. He knew exactly what had to be done. First, he had to prove his data. Gathering was one thing, verifying to everyone's level of belief was another. So: how did Townsend's photos and drawings and descriptions stack up? God bless Townsend, he said: the photos are everything.

Second, he had to place all this in perspective—namely, of the Manhattan Project. Or the Oppenheimer Project. Or the Los Alamos Project. How much would they know of all this? What would a Navy man know?

Third, he had to show how a solution might be found. Sink the German ships in Libreville? Maybe a bad idea, as it would give away our hand. Then the German's would surely know we were on to their atomic bomb project. And Hitler would smell a big fat rat. And he'd then pour all his resources into the bomb.

Or was it even possible to sink those ships in Libreville? The Navy destroyers in the North Atlantic were stretched thin trying to defend the convoys to England. Nobody wanted to admit it, but the German wolf packs were winning the 'Battle of the Atlantic.' What if we sent a flotilla of destroyers down to the Congo to sink some German merchantmen while U-boats were given a free pass to decimate the convoys to Great Britain?

Or, to put it another way, Donovan thought, how many times does the Navy make decisions based on physicists calculating the projected chemical reactions of unstable elements?

Trenton passed by, then Philadelphia, and now there was a straight shot down the line. Donovan wondered if there was any kind of monkey wrench that the OSS could throw into the Germans' plans. Monkey wrench — that was the project name. No — he didn't even bother to write on the pad. The Navy was big on names for projects. So was everybody else. Names send a message — of urgency, of purpose.

Donovan scribbled away as the Express seemed to gain momentum as it hurtled through the fishing villages of Pennsylvania and finally Maryland. Suddenly he looked up from his scribbling and heard the announcement, 'Next: Union Station, Washington.' He was unprepared: full of data, but lacking in direction. What could Townsend do, what could any of his agents do, to take on this train of uranium relentlessly heading toward Hamburg as his Express was heading toward D.C.?

He was lost in thought as he headed to the cab line outside the station. Then a familiar voice brought him up short. "Bill! What the hell took you so long?" It was Stimson. Always the prim gentleman, except when with less than prim gentlemen.

The two men jumped into the back seat of a brown Army car, waiting for them with engine idling. "This is it," Donovan said. "I've got the goods. I aint crying wolf, Henry."

"I can tell," Stimson said. "I've already talked to the Navy guys."

"Yeah?"

"No go. You don't know how thin we're stretched."

"So what'm I here for?"

"Donovan, I'm going to tell you something that I can tell to any other guy. I mean it."

"Shoot. I've got to hear this one."

"What do you do when you're backed into a corner? Do you say, I guess I give up? Or do you get real creative!"

The Army car pulled up to the tennis courts in front of the White House. "Thanks, Sergeant," Stimson said. We can walk from here."

Neither man said anything as they headed toward Pennsylvania Avenue and the entrance to the President's quarters. Donovan could take it no longer. "We're going to the White House?"

"OK, stop right here. Can I tell you what we're up against in the Pacific? We're getting our ass kicked. Do you think we're going to sit here and say 'We give up?'"

"Henry, don't lecture me. What've you got up your sleeve?"

"We're going to throw a monkey wrench at those Japs! We're going to punch them in the nose and see how it bleeds."

"What the hell are you talking about?"

"OK, Donovan, you and your OSS should know this, because right now only the boss and I know it. We're going to bomb Tokyo...."

Donovan smiled a broad Irish smile, as if to say, you two Wall Street types, you two Connecticut Yankees, you two Boston Brahmins, you two Yalies, you two.... You came up with this? "Don't tell me, but what are you going to bomb Tokyo with — a dive bomber?"

"No. B-24s."

"Henry...."

"We've got Jimmy Doolittle out there in San Francisco Bay training these guys to fly B-24s off of aircraft carriers. Impossible, right? Ask Doolittle."

Donovan was never a pilot, never a carrier man. But he knew what this meant. The two men stood in front of the White House, in a clearing, almost Spring day. There was a long silence, as if too much had been discussed, without enough time to take it in. Donovan said, "This is brilliant, beyond anything I could have dreamed up. Did you..."

"Came out of a poker game with Roosevelt. It was a sort of campaign punch in the gut. Make 'em pay, he said. And I took it from there. And Doolittle said it could be done. And the Navy agreed, even though it's Army aircraft."

"What a great propaganda deal!"

"No," Stimson said. "You don't remember that I was in the embassy in Tokyo for 12 years. Or it seemed like twelve! I know those people. They revere the emperor. They think they're better than anybody on earth. Heard that line somewhere before?

"What's your point?"

"I told Roosevelt we've got to insult the emperor. That's all. Then all hell will break loose. They'll do anything to avenge this. They'll throw their game plan overboard. That's all it is. Think about it: just get them to throw their game plan overboard and they'll come to us.'

"Henry, I'll say it again. Brilliant."

"So now it's up to you to think of something brilliant to get the Germans off their game plan."

The two men resumed their walk to the entrance to the White House. They paused at the gate. "Are any ideas germinating in your brain?" Stimson asked with measured seriousness.

"As a matter of fact, yes." Donovan pulled his legal pad out of his valise and sketched an outline of a ship. "The German merchantman that'll be loaded with uranium ore is about the size of the ships we're building for the British. Now there's a Q-boat in on this action. My man down there tells me it has a large crew, too—maybe 400 men. Why? It must be just for shore duty—loading all those trucks with ore. I do know something about ships that size, Henry. They're vulnerable. All that manpower means a lot of accommodations, mess, and so forth. Not a very efficient fighting vessel."

"So what'dya think?"

"All we have to do to disrupt these guys is throw a ship of similar size at 'em. Well-gunned, of course. But a well-manned ship can out gun an over-populated ship any day."

"Keep going."

"I'd like to arm a merchantman of our own—maybe a Liberty ship like the kind that Kaiser's building out on the West Coast. And just run that baby right into the the friggin' krauts."

"Like Doolittle over Tokyo?"

"Yeah."

Stimson thought for a moment. "You give me a code name for this project, and I'll run it right up the flagpole."

"I wouldn't be stealing your name if I used a word from the rising sun project, would I?"

"Not at all. Let's hear it!"

"Code Red."

TWENTY-FIVE

April 4, 1942, Richmond, California

Like the second girl friend, or the second baby, the second ship coming down the ways has a special place in the heart. It's the favored one, the one well considered — favored because wanted for its own sake, and not just to get going. And it was a beauty.

The *Stephen Hopkins* had the tubbish look of its older sister, the first born — broad of beam, rounded fore and aft. Mr. Kaiser himself took pride in it. He planted his considerable girth on the reviewing stand to watch it slowly but ineluctably slip down into the Bay. Around him were all the politicians of the city he could muster on a Monday morning. Yet he had added another element, not seen before, as the champagne bottle with its fancy ribbons banged against the gray metal hull. That ordinary bottle of California bubbly was swung by a woman in overalls. And behind her, rubbing elbows with the politicos, were her cohorts in plaid woolens and jumpsuits and Levis: the distaff welders.

Henry relished the contrast on the stand, as it mirrored the contrast in the water: no sleek cruiser here — no sinister submarine. A merchantman! That was all. And what was wrong with that, especially as such tubs were being torpedoed with increasing regularity all across the Atlantic. The shipyards from the Caribbean to the North Atlantic could scarcely keep up with the daily reports of sinkings. And on the West Coast every available ship had already been commandeered for the 'war effort.'

Even the *Harvard* and the *Yale*, aging relics from World War I service on the Eastern seaboard, then passenger ships with daily sailings between San Francisco and Los Angeles, were now converted into troop ships. It was a good thing, said the owner of the ferry boat line, that wars came so close together, or otherwise there wouldn't be enough ships still seaworthy to get back into uniform.

This April day was a typical one for the Bay: early morning fog, clearing by Noon. Henry Kaiser asked his workers to join him in the 'executive' dining room upstairs for a birthday party: 'all afternoon shifts are cancelled.' As usual, he had an idea behind the celebration.

The menu cards at each space at the tables had been mimeographed with pertinent 'birth' statistics: weight — 7,182 tons; height — raked stem to elliptical stern — 422 feet 9-1/2 inches. Henry joked that a baby's weight never mentioned capacity — who knew? But the *Stephen Hopkins* could carry 314,960 gallons of bunker oil, enough to take her 18,000 miles without refueling. Some baby.

"Now how about mother and father?" he asked with feigned concern. "Ladies and gentlemen, you are the mothers and fathers. And from now on I want you who worked on these ships to keep track of 'em. Through their infancy. Into their terrible twos. Maybe they'll eventually become... teenagers!"

It was another typical Kaiser performance. The women welders were getting a little tired of it. The homeyness was wearing thin. But the baked beans and hamburgers were good, so they stifled their skepticism and listened as if eager to hear the next outpouring.

"Now I know," he began — every sentence from him seemed to begin with 'now' — "this is just a great big fuzzy analogy. But a lot of ships are going to come down these ways, and I want everyone of you to be proud of what you put into them. No one here can possibly do all the paperwork. God knows we don't have that kind of staff. What I'm asking is just that some one of you 'adopt' each one of these ships and follow it. That's right, *follow it.*"

The women and scattering of men at the long tables nodded to each other. Yeah, we can do that, they seemed to acknowledge. But they knew he was hardly done. He seldom left little details hanging.

"So, for example, I'm going to appoint Maria O'Hara to *adopt* the Hopkins. Maria O'Hara, are you here? Would you do us the honor of taking on this new duty?"

The younger women around the room had already sized up Mrs. O'Hara as an 'elder' of the welders. They knew she had a son. She talked often about the Maritime Academy, and how her son was doing there. They also knew she was smart. She took charge of labor disputes over conditions on the docks, the refuse, the lack of toilets. She could argue as a mature woman, even though she hadn't entered the workforce much sooner than any of the others. At least she could speak with authority about how the canning companies in the Valley had cleaned up their work spaces to make them more palatable to women. Nevertheless, Maria was taken by surprise, even anger over the brash assumption that she would undertake such a task.

Maria rose to her feet and fumbled with her napkin. She realized he meant it as an honor. In a flash she had her answer. "As long as it's reflected in my paycheck, sir!" she shot back.

"You're right," he answered with characteristic sureness. "Maria, you, and any of you who adopt these ships as they come down the line, will be paid to keep records on them." He flipped through a few pages on his clipboard and came back with typical brashness, "The Certificate of Registry for *Stephen Hopkins* is in the name of Mr. E. C. Mausshardt, agent of the War Shipping Administration. We've sold it to him, and as soon as it's outfitted with guns and mess tables and refrigerators and stoves and all the other things that make a ship habitable, he will become the new owner."

Maria O'Hara stood awkwardly at the table, proud that she had, once again, told the boss what to do, but uncertain about what she was getting into. "Give me those papers, please," she said warily. "I'll start with Mister what's his name…."

"Mausshardt."

"Yeah, Mausshardt. But, now, who'll tell me what's happening to the ship?"

"I will. Every report I get from now on about *Stephen Hopkins* I'll send to you. I won't bore you with what Mister Mausshardt has to say."

"Bore me...."

The tables were set with several sheet cakes, a candle on each. Henry Kaiser ate with his workers. His staff, including his eldest son, wondered aloud to him about the effectiveness of this sort of camaraderie. He shrugged the comments off. He simply liked people, he told them. You don't realize, he loved to say, how much incompetence rises to the top. When he went back to his corner office, he stared out the window at his new 'baby,' already ringed with small craft bringing material aboard. He knew it would be another month, perhaps, before the ship was ready to sail. In the meantime, what was going on out there, beyond the Golden Gate?

He pulled open his lower desk drawer and removed a bottle of Jim Beam. He was hardly a drinker, surely not a fashionable Scotch or martini drinker. But he loved a slug every now and then. He had had more than a few at the Grand Coulee Dam, when someone always had an excuse for later deliveries of rebar or even the rebar ties. This time it wasn't out of frustration. It was just to slow down his pulse.

He thought for a minute about the bottle atop his desk. The hell with it, he told himself. He went to the water cooler and filled a paper cup halfway. He cracked the Beam and filled the cup to the top. Out there, somewhere, an aircraft carrier was heading across the Pacific, and he knew what it meant. He had been there, just across the Bay at Alameda, when *USS Hornet* steamed away in the early fog with a blanket of tarpaulins across its deck. Underneath were two-engined bombers, B-24 Marauders. These weren't carrier aircraft, the captain agreed with him. These were attack planes. An Army General named James Doolittle was planning to use them on a special mission in the far Pacific. "I can't tell you what the mission is, Mr. Kaiser," the Admiral said, "but I know you'll be very, very happy to find out when it happens."

One of the perks of being connected to the military, to the planners in Washington, Henry thought. The carrier had been gone at least a week. Something would happen within the next week. In his sly way, Henry Stimson had told him as much. But what was it? He got up from his desk and refreshed his drink. He had told the welding crew to take the afternoon off, but he could hear the cranes still working down below. Perhaps his little pep talk had moved them to another level. No matter. The afternoon sun was thin and lifeless on the stiff surface of the Bay.

His first two ships from the Richmond yards were on their way to reaching the Pacific. They were going to carry the war to the Japanese as much as any battleship. They may be armed only defensively. They may never be able to attack another vessel, assault any beachhead. But they will carry the weapons that *will*.

He had enough to drink now. He felt better about challenging his workers, asking them to "adopt" his ships. As his nerves loosened, he felt better about that whimsical decision. After all, in whimsicality he was not alone. Maybe this was the way to exist in a crazy world.

He remembered one silly thing Stimson had told him. He and Roosevelt had read James Hilton's books, among other novels of recent vintage. They enjoyed the same literary allusions. And this is where they got their code names. But this venture, involving an aircraft carrier the Japanese had no idea existed, and aircraft no one had ever associated with a carrier, had an unusual code name. It was pure make believe. And because it was such make-believe, it might even work. Roosevelt's name was enough to blunt the most inquisitive of reporters' questioning. Where were the planes heading? The answer was simple.

Shangri-La.

TWENTY-SIX

May 14, 1942, Long Beach, California

As his merchantman arrived in the Southern California port from San Francisco Bay at his first on-loading stop, Captain Paul Buck had already gained confidence in his crew of 40 sailors and "armed guards" provided by the U.S. Navy. Although it had taken a special Act of Congress to allow Navy personnel to serve on merchant vessels, it was obvious by now that this was a bare minimum of protection against U-boats and enemy surface vessels. This breakdown cruise was short and convincing. *Stephen Hopkins* handled well and at 11 knots wasn't a tug.

The first night out, Captain Buck entertained the Navy personnel, cramped in the top deck staterooms, with wine and cheese. Now, the morning after, it was down to business. The Douglas corporation loading docks were plainly visible from the harbor. There was no mistaking the DBS 'Dauntless' dive bombers lined up along Highway 1. The 'S' was for Scout, but that name didn't do justice to the powerful look of this unique aircraft. And there was little secrecy about the main purpose of these planes "with the holes in their wings." If an enemy agent had wished to examine the "mailed fist of the U.S. Navy," all he had to do was show up along the Coast Highway and take a few snapshots.

In full few of anyone for miles around, these dive bombers had been tested day after day to get as close as possible to a vertical dive. *Aviation Week* reported that the German Stuka was terribly overrated. Yes, it came screaming down with a 500-pound bomb nestled in a cradle between its gull-like wings. But it never achieved more than a skip-bomb type of approach—about 60 degrees. It hit its defenseless targets simply by coming in as close to the ground as possible.

The U.S. Navy couldn't afford to be so complacent. They had to hit ships on ocean, not trucks or train tracks in a straight line on the ground. And those ships would be maneuvering this way and that and well protected with anti-aircraft batteries. So the Navy dive-bombers had to spiral down on their targets like cork screwing hawks. The way to do this, the Douglas master designer discovered by trial and error, was to punch holes in the trailing air flaps of the planes so air could easily flow throw those ailerons as they were laid flat out to hold the aircraft in as vertical a dive as possible. Otherwise, the flaps kept causing violent vibrations that threatened to shake the plane apart. Hence, the local cynics said, the Navy's best aircraft is already full of holes.

The loading process was simple: trucks were driven aboard and lifted to the hold; aircraft had to be tied down above deck. There was enough other ballast, picked up before leaving San Francisco Bay. But the dive bombers were special: they were light and somewhat delicate. After they were secured, the vessel took on the look of a mystery ship. In the early morning, *Hopkins* left Long Beach with the sense of mystery intact. They were headed for Bora Bora, everyone knew. No crew members were allowed off over night. Yet the docks along the harbor were crowded with reporters and the inquisitive. Something big had happened, and everyone wondered if this ship might be a part of it.

What had happened, while *Hopkins* was being outfitted and making its breakdown cruise, was that the U.S. Navy and the U.S. Army had collaborated in the unimaginable: a bombing raid on Tokyo. The Navy had supplied an aircraft carrier; the Army Air Force a fleet of specially equipped two-engine bombers, able to take off a carrier. They had sailed just close enough to the Japanese mainland to strike without arousing enemy defenses, either in the air or on the ground. Unfortunately, a last-minute sighting of the carriers by a Japanese fishing vessel — perhaps a scout? — had forced the planes to take off at too great a distance to continue all the way to safe haven in China. The fate of the planes was unknown.

President Roosevelt took the reporters' questions in the Oval Office of the White House. Yes, he acknowledged, the U.S. had bombed the Japanese capital. He said it with just the right pauses to indicate that the U.S. capital was immune. He left the rest of the story up to speculation. Would there be more? What was the purpose? The only response he made to a direct question was simple enough. Where did the planes come from, and where were they going? One word: Shangri-La.

As *Hopkins* left Long Beach harbor with equally obvious aircraft tied down aboard deck, the speculation grew. Was the U.S. finally taking the war to the Japanese? The crew aboard the tub, the merchantman, was hardly prepared to answer. Among its forty or so men were a mixed group: two Greeks, an Irish citizen, a Swede, a Dane, and a Spanish survivor of the Civil War in his own country. The oldest was a 60-year-old, the youngest a recent graduate of the Maritime Academy, but a man who had already made his way onto a Matson cruise ship to Hawaii, 18-year-old Edwin Joseph O'Hara.

Captain Buck had accepted the fact that the Navy personnel, the "gunners," would be somewhat out of his command, but he hadn't counted on the three civilians who came aboard at Long Beach. They were Douglas company consultants, they told him, and showed their credentials. They were there to assure the proper handling of the SBDs. The staterooms on the upper deck had to do double duty. Buck did his best to fit them in.

Two weeks of loading and outfitting and preparing for unexpected guests, and they were ready to sail — finally. It was June 1, a propitious date.

Once at sea, problems of war and peace and crowded accommodations vanished. The May and June South Pacific weather was calm, unlike the famous wild March winds of the English Channel. Buck had been there, a decade ago, before the war. He knew what his job was: not as much to steer the ship as to know his crew. There was a special bond between the Captain and the least experienced man on board.

There was no concern about radio silence. The route across the South Pacific was somewhat like a Matson Monterey cruise. In the engine room, Edwin O'Hara worked on his training and understanding of this new vessel. He was surprised, one day, to have a personal visit from the Captain. "That's my duty," Buck said, "to keep everyone from bottom to top aware of what a complete team is all about. Maybe you need some gunnery practice."

"I'd love it," O'Hara replied eagerly.

"When we get to Bora Bora. The Japs are doing something very strange."

O'Hara couldn't believe that a senior officer would take any interest in raising a subject like this with a deck hand. He waited.

"Strange maybe is too strong. They're on fire. The Emperor has called for vengeance for the raid on Tokyo. That means they're going to come our way. To Hawaii, maybe."

It was the middle of June, on a steely sea. O'Hara found his bunk as pleasant as the one he had almost two years earlier, on the Mariposa. But what changes had occurred in those two short years: war, armed guards aboard instead of wealthy tourists, planes on deck! He had no idea of where he might post a letter, but he was overwhelmed with the excitement of the steady surge of the *Hopkins* on a military mission and he felt he had to tell someone about it. From the portholes he could see that it was a moonless night. Perhaps his mother had worked on this very ship—how could anyone know?

I'll ask her, he finally told himself. What could the censors object to about that? He undid the compact parcel that held his stationery, and began to write—at first with the hesitance of a freshman in college, but gradually gaining in the confidence of his simple words and the direct meaning he wanted to convey. He was exhilarated, but he was scared. This was no pleasure boat—this was a vessel of war. The guys on board were pretty much the same as those on the *Mariposa*, but more of them were younger, like himself. He could move around the ship, as even the captain had told him to do. But he had to work a longer shift below deck, in the engine room.

Most of all, he was excited about the news of the bombing raid on Tokyo. We were fighting back! Perhaps he could be a part of that fight. He sealed the envelope with that hope lingering above his name, and addressed it to Maria O'Hara, Kaiser Shipyards, Richmond, California.

There would be no mistaking that.

TWENTY-SEVEN

June 21, 1942, Los Alamos, New Mexico

"What in hell are the Germans up to?" General Groves demanded to know, as he opened his weekly conference meeting. "They're way ahead of us on the science. They've got rockets. They're getting their asses kicked in Russia. Why aren't they building the bomb?"

Robert Oppenheimer knew he was expected to answer for his scientists, his kitchen staff, and maybe even for his mistresses. He gave a glassy look at the boss at the head of the table — bulging out of his army uniform, his tie neatly tucked into his shirt, his face ruddy from the high-desert sun and a generous daily stipend of scotch and sodas. Oppie could have answered in the spirit of the question, but he knew that was what the general always wanted. So he answered with an equally speculative question.

"Why aren't they aware of the uranium they need?"

A smile spread over the general's face. He reached down into his government-issue briefcase and pulled up a slim envelope. "I'll ask everyone here at this table to listen carefully. What I'm about to read you is from the Office of Special Services, in Washington. That's the OSS. They have a two-part message. Now, ordinarily, I'd say this is just a way of lighting a fire under us. But Robert has just told us, with his question, why I don't think this is just a 'hurry up.'"

Oppenheimer feigned disinterest. "The OSS, huh?"

"They've got a man tracking Heisenberg. They've got an agent in Stockholm, with Lise Meitner. And now they've got guys in Africa."

The scientists around the table usually deferred to Oppenheimer, but now Ulam spoke up. "How in the devil do they follow Heisenberg? He's all over Germany."

"Not my job to know. But let me read you the message. None of this goes beyond this room, right?" He looked at each man and then ceremoniously undid the flap on the envelope. "Bill Donovan is nobody's fool. I've known him for a dozen years. He gets right to the point. Number one: Heisenberg is taking over from Hahn. They're moving out of Berlin. Probably to somewhere along the Rhine. They need lots of water, for cooling. And they need tons of uranium, and that means they have to move it on barges, not trains."

"Barges? How're we getting it here?"

"Nobody's bombing *our* trains — yet."

"OK. What's Number two?"

"As I said, Africa. That's right: they're getting their U-238 from the Congo. They've had raiders and cargo ships in French Equatorial Africa for a month now."

Oppenheimer knew when to agree. "General, this is terrific news, if true. Maybe we can get the guys in Manhattan to ship us the Belgian uranium."

"What do you mean 'Get them'? I'll send the order right now."

"And send the order to sink the German ships...."

"And tell Santa Claus. You tell me when you need the uranium from Manhattan, and I'll have it on the next train out of Penn Station."

Oppenheimer opened his notebook and pencilled in some notes. Ulam and Seligman made faces as if to jump into the discussion, but held back. Finally, Oppenheimer tossed his notebook on the table and delivered his verdict: "We're behind schedule. We still don't have the calculations on critical mass from Chicago. I say we ship it little by little, starting ASAP. Then we can stockpile it here and separate out the good from the bad. Gentlemen, this is like shipping fifty tons of horseshit. Let's make sure we have the best horseshit in one fucking place! Now, what's next?"

General Groves got up and went to the telephones outside. The men around the table could hear his orders barked to Washington. "Start shipping the Manhattan stock to

148

Los Alamos. Give me a total quantity and I'll work up a shipping schedule. Got it? Wire me from Manhattan."

"Are we going to sit here speculating about the Germans, or are we going to get this thing done?" Groves said as he reentered the room.

"A little speculation won't hurt," Ulam answered. "It's better to get it right in three days than wrong in two days."

"What's that supposed to mean?"

"Heisenberg will get it wrong."

"So you think we can squander our time.... Oh, I know — we finally gave the Japs a licking. You guys did know this, right? We sunk four of their carriers at Midway."

"We get the papers. Yeah, it was two weeks ago," Seligman confirmed. "That really takes the pressure off."

"Wrong! Nimitz is way understaffed. The Navy is stretched very, very thin."

Ulam nodded. "No matter how the war goes in the Pacific, the danger is in Germany."

Oppenheimer wanted to break in, but he saw that the young mathematician from Poland was speaking for *his* way of thinking, too. Heisenberg had made his reputation at the height of the quantum revolution in Europe, in the late 1920s. His 'principle of indeterminacy' made his reputation. It was a time when reputations could be made by outrageous claims — or even, as in this case, modest claims with outrageous names. Schroedinger had no qualms about writing his acceptance speech for his Nobel prize — in poetry. The new science was full of ideas that the man in the street found mystical. Einstein's upside-down 'relativity' universe of 1918 set the table. Now every science writer was eating it up.

Ulam looked to Oppenheimer for a brief moment, then saw he had the table. He ran with it. "If they've taken it away from Strassman and Hahn, and handed it off to Heisenberg, they're going in the wrong direction. They need to go to a plumber, not a philosopher. Now, Lise Meitner — she's a plumber — but she refuses to help anybody build a bomb."

"Robert, what's your take on this?" Groves shot back.

"Mr. Ulam has been there. Unless the OSS knows more than they're telling us, we have a great chance to beat 'em. But only if —"

"Only if what?"

"Only if we cut off their uranium supply. Once they get enough of that stuff, they'll blunder into a bomb!"

"Yeah?"

"They'll realize that a critical volume is necessary. *We* know that. Our only hope is that *they're* just guessing."

General Grove rose to sign off on the meeting. Ulam walked outside quickly, embarrassed about his confrontation with the chief. Oppenheimer joined him. It was too early for lunch, too late for any meaningful work. They walked to the flagpole that had been hastily erected in the center of the compound. Why is it that any enterprise requires a center, a tower of some sort, a symbol of authority? Who knew? It just made sense to have a location around which the wheel spun. They looked out over the vast plain of New Mexico that was heating up below in the hard sunlight, on this, the first day of summer. The vista spoke back to them: the world is more important than you.

Oppenheimer opened up first, ignoring what was clearly on his younger friend's mind. "You'll have to trust me on this one — we're not going to let the Germans get that uranium."

"I didn't know you were clued in to the military—"

"I'm not. But I have a connection in Berkeley...."

General Groves suddenly came up behind them, as if suspecting the two had an understanding he was unaware of.

"Berkeley, you say? May I join you?"

"General, I've got a wife out there..."

"Oh, I thought—"

"...and some good friends on the Cal rugby team. You'd be surprised what gentlemen you meet on a rugby team."

"Yes?"

"And you'd be surprised what you can learn from them."

Groves knew enough about his charismatic director of atomic bomb project not to push him too far. But he sensed, once again, he was the outsider. He, the general, who paid the bills and ran interference in Washington, had to cow-tow to this — this — this infuriating playboy. Just what did he mean about a rugby player in Berkeley?

"Robert, you're being poetic again," he said with a wan smile. "Can you be a little more prosaic — for my sake?"

"General, I'm just guessing. I'll tell you all I know. The OSS has recruited a guy that I used to follow on the Cal rugby team. That same guy, it seems, is heading up the effort to throw a monkey wrench in the German bomb program. Ironic, isn't it — two guys from Cal, on opposite sides of the world, one trying to make a bomb, the other trying to kill it."

Groves was satisfied. "When the time comes, you'll tell me his name — OK?"

TWENTY-EIGHT

Berchtesgarten, Munich, June 21, 1942

The summer sun would reach its finest orbit in southern Germany toward the beginning of July. Hitler had preferred late Spring for his vacation here, but setbacks on the Russian front had delayed this year's visit. Besides which, there were more pressing things than vacations, he had scarcely to tell himself. Yet here was the vista that had unfolded before him many times before, and had engulfed him in a certain pride of country.

Hitler didn't realized the significance of the date of his arrival — by train from Berlin — until a radio at his summer home suddenly filled the lobby of his complex with the strains of the Star Spangled Banner. It was six P.M. here, or late morning in the U.S. Straight from Washington, D.C., the announcer said: "in training for a parade up the Capitol Mall, with fireworks and speeches, to be held in about two weeks, on the day of independence, there will be new celebrations with undiminished fervor here in the Nation's capital, even in this time of obvious crisis." Hitler listened to the end of the anthem, surprised that a country newly at war would turn to fireworks to celebrate just the anticipation of a national holiday.

This was no vacation, however. The heads of each Wehrmacht department were already at the conference room in Hitler's private villa, none of them sure of what to expect from the Fuhrer. They knew the routine: quick reports, some questioning, then a late dinner. Perhaps some good news to ease the tension of almost three years of war.

As soon as Hitler entered the room, Admiral Doenitz passed some papers to him. He was senior enough to challenge the usual protocol, especially in the informal atmosphere of Hitler's retreat.

"Always the good news first, eh, Herr Doenitz? May we say the era of the battleship is over?"

"In the Atlantic, yes!"

"And why not the Pacific, too? What is the lesson of the battle at Midway last month?"

Goebbels liked the way the meeting was opening. He volunteered, "They're not fighting sea battles with guns any more. With planes."

"Right."

"Or with torpedoes," Doenitz objected. "Give us six more good months and we'll starve England."

"But I ask the question again. What does Midway mean to *us*?"

"That Japan has failed us," Himmler shot back. "We counted on Yamamoto, that genius, to push the Americans back to Australia. And what does he do? He tries to repeat Pearl Harbor. What an idiot!"

Hitler raised his hand to call the meeting to order. "Let's come back to that, Herr Himmler. But for now, I want an accounting of where we stand. What do we know from Rommel?"

Von Rundstedt had recently returned from command on the Russian front, but was without a specific assignment in the West. Though he had presided over the successful envelopment of France in 1940, he was suspected of "letting the British off the hook" in the evacuation of Dunkirk. Hitler may have wanted to sign a peace treaty with England, but if he thought this would be the right signal he completely misread Winston Churchill. The old general knew it was he who had to answer Hitler's question about Rommel. He was the only one with a sense of reality. Everyone around the table knew it.

"Rommel has been stopped on his run toward Cairo," Von Rundstedt answered, pretending to check his notes. "At

El Alamein. Montgomery changed his strategy and was able to confine our panzers...."

"What do you mean 'confine our panzers'?! I've never heard anything like this!"

"He held back and let our panzers power right in. It was sheer force. They just had more armor on the ground. The damn Brits just threw up a ring around us, and we couldn't break out. Without being able to maneuver, we lost our advantage."

Hitler rose from the table and walked to a bank of maps hung along the side of the room, like a giant tapestry. "So what you're saying is we lost the battle at El Alamein."

"It's still going on, last I heard. Rommel was lucky to save most of his tanks. He's regrouping. But I would say he's not going to have a beer in Cairo any time soon"

Hitler stabbed at an area in Africa, and removed a series of pins. There were large circles in red and black across the semicircle from Norway to Egypt. "Gentlemen, we are not yet three years into this war and we're hitting a wall. A wall! Leningrad — what a stinking mess! This is the twentieth century and we're conducting a siege! Sieges! That's the middle ages."

Herman Goering was close enough to his boss to protest. "Give me the airplanes we wasted on London and I'd have Leningrad in a week. But we have our priorities..."

"Moscow? Is that what you mean?"

"We can't get the fuel to Moscow to put on a fucking flying circus."

"And Stalingrad?" the Fuhrer continued petulantly.

Von Rundstedt had had enough. "If the winter turns out as bad next month as it did at Moscow, we're going to lose half our army down there. My son is in that army. And so are four hundred thousand other good sons...."

Hitler closed his eyes as if to contain his anger. "General, I don't have any sons. Or, I should say, I have several million sons..."

"Everyone of them you allow to be killed is one less we have to fight with." The room was uncomfortably silent. Even Von Rundstedt could go too far with the Fuhrer. "Perhaps," he continued, "I'm talking like an old fool. But I feel it in my bones. Time's not on our side."

"You said it. You *are* an old fool!" Hitler paced back and forth, to let his vitriol sink in. Finally: "But at least you speak your mind. What's wrong with the rest of you old maids? Lost your tongues?"

Goering hazarded a guess. "Ask us something about what we know, and we'll answer. But you're the only one here, Adolph, who knows what's going on in the big picture." His tone was just obsequious enough to avoid a curse. Even Hitler understood that Goering was close to being right.

"At least I can add," Von Rundstedt said. "We dealt with Poland, then France, then Norway. We beat the shit out of Britain. We had the Russians running. Greece, Crete, North Africa."

"Crete! Can you imagine?" Hitler broke in. "Riefenstahl wanted to make a movie about that boxer — what's his name? So he's a paratrooper in Crete—"

"So he beat Joe Louis," Goebbels said. "I turned her down."

"Anyway. Yeah, we had 'em running. Now what?"

Goering jumped at the chance to bring Hitler's favorite subject back. "The big bomb," he said.

"Right! Not big bomb. *The* bomb."

"I have a report on that," Goering said. "We've got the material coming from Africa. Admiral?"

Doenitz nodded. "From the horn of Africa. It's uranium, to be accurate. All it takes is one full shipload and a raider to cover it. We've got a crew of a couple hundred men from both ships just bringing the stuff in from the mines."

"Good! When will it be here?"

"We made a first run already. Heisenberg and his guys checked it out. It passed. Now comes the big delivery."

"When? That's what I asked, damn it. When?"

"In September. "

"You control the sea lanes down there?"

"Better than anywhere. The Brits are fighting for their lives to get convoys in to their little green island. The Americans are up to their necks in the Pacific. The South Atlantic is like a swimming pool for the kiddies."

Hitler returned to the table and sat down jauntily in his chair. "Gentlemen, this is one piece of news that can change all the rest of the war fronts. One bomb, that's all I ask. And they'll be begging to make peace. It doesn't have to be the destruction of London. Maybe I'd like to visit London some day. It could be the Suez Canal. It could be Switzerland — no, that's where our bankers are. Ah, I know — Moscow. It'll be a knockout."

Himmler lit up. "A knockout. That's it. That's the guy who decked Joe Louis. Max Schmeling."

Von Rundstedt bit his lip. "We're not going to win this war with propaganda. Either we win on the field or we fold the tent. You talk about the bomb. That's your ace in the hole. I have to agree. Churchill will never make peace with us when he realizes we've been stopped on the field."

"Churchill! That little toad! Gentlemen, this meeting is over. I want Heisenberg down here tomorrow with a direct report. Himmler — you get him here if you have to squeeze his nuts."

Himmler smiled. "He'll be here."

TWENTY-NINE

June 21, 1942, Bora Bora, Fiji Islands

The American freighter rose above the tiny harbor like an ocean liner on a Mississippi River town. The *Stephen Hopkins* anchored off shore, well away from the coral reefs that ringed the lagoon. In a little more than six months, this Polynesian outpost of France had become a major supply center for U.S. military deliveries to the South Pacific. To the forty or so men aboard *Hopkins*, the twin volcanic mountains and the coconut trees that lined the harbor looked like a textbook vision of a peaceful ocean atoll — a place where French artists set up their easels in the days before world wars.

Except for the armaments. Partially hidden in the vegetation on the mountain sides were concrete abutments whose six-inch cannon barrels glistened in the island's mists. War was the new reality, not art.

Captain Paul Buck gave his crew an all-on-deck pep talk before sending them ashore. "This is the best three weeks, gentlemen, I've had at sea in all my career. You are a great crew. Maybe we thought we saw a periscope here and there. Our gunners were ready. Maybe our speed wasn't much better, it seemed, than a canoe on Lake Tahoe. But our engine department made it seem easy. The Seabees are how going to take over. They'll take those beautiful dive bombers ashore. And when *you all* go ashore, I want you to make our ship proud. Get back on time. Don't waste your money on anything you'd be ashamed of later. Have a few beers — I know you will. But remember — you're Americans, and we're fighting a war."

The Naval armed guards and the odd passengers on board remained with Captain Buck while dinghies were lowered for the crew. The Seabees came aboard from barges and went about unloading the cargo with unaccustomed caution. They had never seen a ship quite like this. Oh, it was a merchantman, but it had 50 caliber machinegun buckets fore and aft and a 4-inch cannon midships. There were army cannons on the bridge, along with further machine guns. The ship had heft, in overall size and in its steel hull. This was no greyhound, any Seabee could tell, but neither was it a patsy.

In the village that surrounded the make-shift port of the lagoon, the crew of *Stephen Hopkins* presented another view of the American presence on the island. U.S. Navy and Army personnel of all ranks filled the one long commercial street of the village. They were bivouacked all over the island, mainly around the Seabee-built airstrip, but in their free hours they spent what little curiosity they had on the mixture of French and native culture "in town." Edwin O'Hara and his merchant marine buddies felt a sense of pride in mixing with their uniformed compatriots.

Captain Buck had sized up his crew well on the two-week voyage to Bora Bora. There were enough seasoned mariners to be a counterpoint to the 'kids' from the Academy. Poker games were kept to a minimum — there just wasn't enough money to make it interesting. But several of the old-timers had chess sets, and there was nothing like a long, monotonous trip to allow plenty of time for board games. Neither did Buck try to over-manage his crew: there was no need to stay on board every night while in port. He knew well that temptation was tempered by two things: Navy men, who had been in Bora Bora for months, had done their best to soak up the pleasure spots on the island; and the merchant marine fellows had neither the flare nor the cash to compete for what was left. As a result, most of the crew made their way back to *Hopkins* after a few hours of wandering through the commercial district of the town — even on the first night of their visit.

Engine mate O'Hara spent enough time on shore to buy some picture postcards to include in a letter he had long planned. Mail to the states went off on a regular schedule, with a delivery time of about three weeks. He could just catch his girl friend's birthday, of mid-July. It was also a day of distinct memories in their brief romance — of that day on her uncle's boat in San Francisco Bay, now almost three years ago. But, he thought — what did it matter? — we'll be on our way back to Richmond in a few days, and might even beat the mail home. Well, it did matter: letters written from afar, even if they arrive after the writer does, carry the magic of distance. Just distance: the magic of putting thoughts on paper as if intended for history, the aura of two worlds apart.

On the third morning in Bora Bora, *Hopkins* was ready to leave port. The Captain assembled everyone on deck at six o'clock. He thanked them for maintaining the honor of the merchant marine: there were no problems reported in port. Then, without a hint of seriousness, he asked if everyone had put their letters home in the Navy mailbox on shore. Of course, the silence said. "I'm asking this," Captain Buck said, "because we're not going straight back to the states."

The radio operator, Hudson Hewey, a veteran of the service, was confused. He had been passing around tidbits of news to the crew over the voyage so far, and there was nothing to indicate a change in the course of the war so far. Midway was the big event. It had taken the pressure off the defense of Australia. Four line carriers of the Japanese Navy were now on the bottom of the Pacific. The U.S. had finally lost *Yorktown*, the carrier that had taken the last hit it could handle. *Hornet* was badly damaged from the Midway battle, and would spend the next year in drydock in Seattle — or maybe in San Francisco, which it had left on track of its decisive raid on Tokyo. Only *Enterprise* was still afloat. The Japanese were hurting, but they still heavily outnumbered the U.S. and were in control of carrier operations. Ensign Hewey had all the facts at his disposal. He felt it was his duty to comment on the Captain's plans.

"What's changed, Captain?" he asked innocently. "Are we going to pick up some freight somewhere else?"

"I don't mind your asking. We might. But we're really just heading to Australia."

"Australia!"

"Yes. Orders from Washington."

"But that's another week or so away."

"No one's hiding that. I just want everybody to know this is a major change of plans. You can write home again when we get there."

The radio operator knew Buck wouldn't mind his next question. "Captain, are we actually going to see some action? I've heard we're invading Guadalcanal."

"You know as well as I do. We have a beachhead there. But we're not going there. OK? Now, let's pull anchor and get the hell out of here."

THIRTY

Robert Oppenheimer's hillside home above the University of California campus was an ideal place for a conference. It was also easier to get to than Los Alamos, Australia, or even Washington, D.C. These were the locations that mattered for this particular meeting. Each was represented with one visitor.

As expected, the genial host didn't deviate from his accustomed offer of dry martinis all round. From Melbourne, the merchant marine and the U.S. Navy were represented by Vice Admiral William Taylor. From Washington, the O.S.S. had designated George Townsend to present their case. Miroslav Ulam was the numbers man from Los Alamos. The most unlikely man to oversee a meeting of such military importance was the martini maker. But he had one big advantage over all the rest: he alone knew what everyone there *knew.*

Each of the three men, in turn, accepted Oppenheimer's offer out of a ceremonial politeness. Then Townsend went to the refrigerator for a beer, Taylor switched to ice water, and Ulam spotted a bottle of shlibowitz in the kitchen and poured himself a good toke. Now it was down to business.

Townsend began with a notebook presentation, as was his wont, flipping page over page as if they were 20"x30" pages on an easel. The point was obvious: he had been there — in Stockholm, in Libreville, in Washington, in New York. Even in Richmond, California. Or, maybe, especially there.

Point number one: the Germans had finally understood the necessity of large quantities of uranium, or even plutonium — if they could get it. They had run a sample of the uranium ores from Libreville. They were ready to muscle a huge shipment into Hamburg, from where it work go by trainload to their Rhine reactor facility.

Point number two: the British had no way to stop this shipment. German U-boats controlled all shipping in the Channel. Strategic bombing of the German rails was a failure. There were too many tracks, too few aircraft.

Point number three: the U.S. Navy had no destroyers available to challenge German vessels in the Atlantic. German U-boats were raiding and sinking merchantmen as they came out of Norfolk, Philadelphia, New York, and even Boston. The U.S. Eastern seaboard was a pheasant shoot for Admiral Doenitz's men.

Point number four: even if the U.S. Navy could scrape up a destroyer or two for this mission, what kind of a message would this send to the enemy? Stimson made the point bluntly: don't ever let the enemy know what we're doing, or why we're doing it.

Therefore, Townsend concluded, we've decided to throw a monkey wrench into their plans. And this is why *Hopkins* is headed to Australia and beyond. In fact, the plan is already going ahead.

Vice-Admiral Taylor realized that he was there to ratify, not to reason. No record of the meeting was being kept, he said, but "For the record, I'd like to say this is extraordinary. Surely if this is as critical as you've said, wouldn't an Air Force raid — or some other approach, less cockamamie than this — be our first choice?"

"Good question," Townsend agreed. "We explored an air attack. Do you know what the timing is for that?"

"Worse than sending an iron bucket around the world?"

Oppenheimer liked to change the subject when things got rough — and then come back in the next breath with his point. "My friend tells me that a five hundred pound bomb would surely do the job. Isn't that right, George?"

"Well — if you could guarantee a hit..."

"The hit's the thing, right?"

"Sure. But even with dive bombers operating off an aircraft carrier it's a tough proposition."

"And let's not talk about aircraft carriers, right?"

The Vice-Admiral shrugged. "You've made your point — short of a full-fledged military operation, we're not going to stop that ship."

"One ship?"

"With a raider for protection. That's what we've found out so far." The Vice-Admiral sensed the frustration. "Maybe we should fight fire with fire. If only we could afford a sub to go after 'em."

"Sorry, gentlemen," Townsend said. "We have Henry Stimson on our side, and even he can't free up any kind of Navy help on this one."

"So what you're saying is that it's a fait d'accompli. Is that right?

"That's why our gunboat is in Melbourne, Admiral."

Ulam finally got up the courage to enter the fray. "Admiral — "

"Vice Admiral...."

"Sorry. I do respect proper title. I'd just like to say something. Doctor Oppenheimer brought me here to give you the numbers on that uranium. But I must insist — it isn't just about the shipment...."

"Oh?"

"Put yourself in Hitler's place — "

"Thank you, no!"

"What if we bring in aircraft and a destroyer and sink the damned tub, what does he do?"

"You think he gets his back up?"

"You bet. He says to his gang, 'Why are they so hot to stop us?' And he doesn't wait for an answer."

"Yeah — then we've given away our hand, and we're in for a bigger battle than Stalingrad."

"So you think Hitler doesn't realize the importance of this?"

"Hitler may suspect. But if Heisenberg flops, as I know he will, then you add this to it and Hitler says, 'OK, it's another pipe dream.' Trust me. Heisenberg himself will be happy to flop, and then he'll be off the hook." Ulam threw back the rest of a shot of shlibowitz.

The Vice-Admiral got up from his chair and stretched his legs. "Robert, do you suppose you could fix me one of your patented martinis? You realize, of course, that this is a suicide mission."

"Most likely," Townsend replied at once. "We're essentially putting up a big tub of a merchantman against a heavily laden transport, about the same size, but with ten times the number of men aboard. And that's just the start. The Q-boat has been making this run with the transport."

"So you're going in — down two to one."

"Right. All we have to do is throw in the monkey wrench. We don't have to win the battle."

Oppenheimer returned from the kitchen quickly with a shaker of martinis and a glass for the Vice-Admiral. Taylor put the drink to his lips, turned, and looked out onto the view to the Golden Gate Bridge. The sun was just disappearing into the Pacific. The meeting had gone well enough, Oppenheimer thought. What, after all, could be done, now that the OSS had taken over the mission? All had given their input. The troubling part was the last comment from the Navy man. It was a suicide mission, unless one believed in miracles.

"Mister Townsend," the Vice Admiral said, prolonging the discussion, everyone knew, to fulfill his duty as the senior man there, "what would you say to the men on *Hopkins* about undertaking a suicide mission?"

"I'll tell them to think of it as getting some action."

"When, pray tell, will you do this?"

"When I join them on board."

THIRTY-ONE

July 22, 1942, Melbourne, Australia

The contrast between Bora Bora and this bustling commercial city wasn't lost on Captain Buck. The shock to the crew, he knew, would make them realize this wasn't an ordinary voyage. They had now been in the South Pacific for almost a month, the better part of July. From Bora Bora to Auckland, New Zealand alone took a week. On the way the crew had some time for gunnery practice on North Island. It was a leisurely schedule, almost a vacation for a crew who believed that the South Pacific was infested with rattlesnakes. Radio operator Hewey had become the most popular man on board: he was the only one who seemed to know what was going on in the world at large.

A greater surprise to most of the merchantmen was that mail from the states awaited them in Melbourne. This couldn't happen unless someone, somewhere, was following their itinerary. The captain kept the men on board until supplies were delivered from a U.S. Navy launch. They were low on a little of everything, from general ship's stores to ammunition for their 50-caliber machine guns. A large duffel bag of mail was the final item to be run up the gangplank.

"Give a little credit to your merchant marine," Captain Buck yelled over the incessant noise of the harbor, the tugboats and the ratcheting of the cranes all along the docks. "They can deliver the mail!"

Edwin O'Hara felt no embarrassment at all when his name was called out multiple times for mail. "It's all from my mother," he yelled each time he got the call. "When she isn't welding, she's writing," he explained to Captain Buck and anyone else within earshot, as he accepted the fourth piece.

But the fifth letter appeared to be different. The Captain turned it up to the sun as if he couldn't quite make out the name on it. "It's for you, again, Mr. O'Hara. Something funny about this one...."

The radio operator sensed what the Captain was up to, from long experience. "At last, the girl friend is heard from!"

"Sulfina Androcoles," the Captain said with a broad smile. He waved the envelope in the air before flipping it to O'Hara. "Some moniker! Some girl friend!"

O'Hara went along with the joshing. "Sue, I call her."

The radio operator wouldn't let go: "Let's see which one he opens first!"

"I'll save the best for last...."

"Men," Captain Buck shouted, "let's have some lunch. We're going to be here for a while, according to *my* mail. Assemble here at thirteen hundred hours. I'll give you your orders then. OK? Dismissed!"

O'Hara slipped his letters into his knapsack and went below decks. Why had she used her full Greek name on the envelope? It couldn't be good news, he assured himself: get ready for a letdown. Bound to happen. Out of sight, out of mind. Well, at least she wrote....

"You gonna have some lunch?" his engine room buddy asked.

"I think I'll wait until we go ashore. I'm ready for a beer or two."

"Yeah. Or maybe—"

There was one thing about a ship at sea for any length of time — there were no secrets among the crew. You could go crazy trying to keep a secret. If you didn't like to talk, or you *did* like to talk — it made no difference. It must be something like prison, O'Hara thought: if you don't meet every guy eye to eye you'll make a little prison for yourself. But there was one big difference — you could spend most of your free time with guys like you. The radio operator, Hudson Hewey, was such a guy.

More than twice Edwin's age, Hewey had the survival instincts of an old sea dog — and he didn't mind telling anybody what they were: never volunteer for anything, never force anything, never pick a fight you can't finish. Built like a lightweight boxer, he was always clean-shaven and took pride in his slicked back, black broom of hair. He had a stack of paperback books in his locker, which he loaned to any fellow sailor at the least hint of interest. I'm no do-gooder, he'd say — I'd just like to see if anybody agrees with me about what a good book is. Besides, I'm a poor poker player....

Hewey remained quiet and out of sight as O'Hara opened his letters. The ones from his mother would be long, inquisitive, and upbeat. His own mother, not yet seventy, knew better than to pester him with mail, after all these years at sea. She would answer only when he "opened the conversation." But now, on her son's first assignment, and in a war zone, O'Hara's mother could be expected to show her concern and pride, and four letters over the space of a month and a half seemed about right.

Hewey heard O'Hara get up from the bench and shut his locker. "Done readin'?" he asked.

"All's I need right now."

Hewey couldn't resist. "Mind readin' one of yer letters to me? I aint had one in quite a spell."

O'Hara turned and looked at the radio man. "Not much to read...."

"Aw, com'on. Just a sample...."

O'Hara reopened his locker and retrieved a thin envelope. "My mom's a welder, you know, at Kaiser Shipyard. In Richmond. She actually worked on part of this ship—"

"You mentioned that...."

"OK, here's the best one. Er, part of one. Now, don't laugh—"

"Course not!"

"Here's how it goes: *You'd be proud of me, Eddie. I never thought I could lift a hammer, and now I'm swinging an electric torch up and down a seam between two huge steel plates. I don't know what part of the ship they may be, these things are so huge. We work on wooden platforms maybe thirty feet or so off the ground. You couldn't throw a football as high up as we are....*"

"What a woman! Go on—"

"It's just more of the same. And in the other letters she tells me about her new apartment in Berkeley. She shares it with some of the other women from the shipyard. The Bay stinks like a sewer at this time of the year. But they keep the windows closed."

"Sounds great. Now, how about the letter from your girl friend?"

"Oh, that. I haven't opened it...."

"What?!"

"I thought I'd save it for the first bar in town."

Hewey had now met the younger generation. "Oh. Well then, let's go!"

No sailor was left on board as the skiffs ferried them to the docks. Australian hospitality was legendary in the merchant marine. Scuttlebutt had it that the cheaper bars were at the southern end of the harbor, where the fishing boats congregated. Hewey had his own idea. "I've been in a dozen harbors like this. Walk a little further and find a neighborhood bar." O'Hara followed his friend's advice. Soon they were comfortably ensconced at the end of an empty bar, tended by a sleepy-eyed young woman.

"Where you boys from?" she greeted.

"The states. And eager to try those great beers we've heard so much about. Tap, huh?" Hewey nudged O'Hara as the woman swayed back down the plank to draw two pints. "Nothing like the first sight of a feminine figure after time at sea, eh boy?"

When she returned with two frothy pints, she gave in to a smile, as if to say, thanks for the admiring looks. Hewey smiled back. "Don't mind us staring," he apologized.

"I get it all the time. My honey's at sea, too...."

"Here's to you!" Hewey said. "We're all in the same boat."

"And you, young man," the barmaid ventured, "you seem lost in thought."

"He's just got a letter from his girl friend back home."

"Oh oh. Bad news, eh?"

"He hasn't even opened it!" Hewey laughed.

"Well then, let's do it! It may be great news!"

O'Hara took a long sip of his beer, wiped his mouth. "Guess I should. It's kinda personal, so I'd better read it first."

"Of course...." The bartender shrugged.

O'Hara walked to the window, looking out on a drab street, with the vast harbor just visible over row houses that could have been in Scotland. He opened the letter and read. He could barely contain a smile, and gave a thumbs up sign. He returned to his stool and took another long sip from his glass.

"So?" the bartender asked.

"She's wonderful. She makes more sense than—"

"Edwin, would you mind reading us the letter?" Hewey said. "Maybe *we* could use some good news."

"Well, OK. Part of it. Here's how she ends: *All I ask is you take care of yourself. The news is terrible. Ships are being sunk every day. And I don't care if you fall into bad company and do things you shoudn't. All I care about is you don't fall in love with anybody else but me. Have you got that clear? You are in love with me, and nobody else.*

"That's beautiful," the bartender said. "I'm going to write that to my guy."

Hewey agreed. "Write Sue a letter. Today. And tell her one thing is for sure. *You're coming back.*"

THIRTY-TWO

August 20, 1942, Stockholm, Sweden

George Townsend had one more monkey wrench at his disposal. Wild Bill had put him up to it. Would the Germans be stupid enough to change plans in midstream if a scientific doubt were raised about the bomb? Townsend answered the question. Not the Germans, but Hitler might.

Townsend argued with Donovan that Hitler fit the profile of standard Freudian psychiatry: the narcissist who changed plans on a whim. The whim might be the result of voices heard in the night, or signs from the stars, or simple intuition. The result was the same: decisions that no one could countermand or disagree with because the leader was above dispute. Hitler contained within himself both the certainty of his vision and the certitude of his power. It was the nightmare of omnipotence.

Therefore, Townsend argued, give Hitler a reason to doubt his generals or his scientists and a terribly bad decision would result. It had happened at Dunkirk. The British Expeditionary force could have been slaughtered on the beaches. Von Rundstedt presumably recommended it. But somehow a designing Hitler thought that this act of holding back would endear him to Churchill. Hmmm.

Earlier, in 1940, an even more obvious failure of reason directed the German attack on London, instead of putting the British airfields out of commission north of London. The result was that the RAF won the 'Battle of Britain' even though Hitler relished the sight of the British capital in flames.

How do you expect to get Hitler to question his nuclear scientists? Donovan had asked. It was obviously a tall order. Townsend's answer was based on his experience in

Stockholm, when he was able to get through to Lise Meitner only by using an outrageous disguise. The SS is all over Meitner. They know she's the key to the fission of uranium. That's why they've given up on Strassman and Hahn, and have put Heisenberg in charge. If I can somehow get Meitner to say nuclear bombs are impossible, the news will go to Hitler like a telegram for money.

So go for it! Donovan said. Only this time, I can get you into the U.S. Embassy, and she can meet you there.

The timing was less than perfect. German ships were scheduled to be in Libreville in a little more than a month, to pick up the uranium. But Townsend knew exactly where *Hopkins* was. After a week in Melbourne, the merchantman had raised anchor and headed....around the south of Australia and into the Indian Ocean. At Port Lincoln, on the West coast of Australia, she had taken on some kind of cargo, for ballast. Townsend had become familiar with a certain radioman on *Hopkins* named Hewey. Between Berkeley, New York, and London, Townsend was able to draw his own itinerary and that of *Hopkins.* Already he could put the two routes on a graph and find them intersecting at an unusual place: Durban, South Africa.

Townsend hoped he could complete plan A — Hitler's change of mind — before plan B — a confrontation with the German "UR'-boats," as the OSS had named them. It was another nice touch: "UR-boat" could be mistaken as a typographical error for U-boat. But the basic issue remained: would Hitler cancel the Libreville mission if he gave up on the bomb, or would the uranium get through anyway and just be there on the Rhine for someone like Heisenberg to use it?

Donovan had arranged, this time, for Townsend to have a second identity in Stockholm. The drayage firm that brought ice to the U.S. embassy was politely urged to fit Townsend out as a deliveryman. Fortunately, Townsend was no sooner off the ferry from Copenhagen than a ramshackle truck approached him and the driver told him sternly to jump in.

One change of caps and shirt and the former Cal rugby player was an iceman.

"Our job is just to get you in the Embassy. Stay there as long as you like. But we're leaving before the ice melts." Townsend nodded. A reception was planned for the evening. Just a local formality. Lise Meitner is invited to represent the Institute where she works. Townsend is to remain in the kitchen of the Embassy, until Meitner finds an excuse to join him.

So far, so good, Townsend kept reminding himself as he waited. He tried to imagine what the crew on *Hopkins* was thinking, as they took off on a 4800-mile journey across the Indian Ocean. Worse, what was the Captain thinking about explaining this to his crew? You're supposed to be delivering essential materiel to the stretched-thin U.S. forces in the South Pacific. And you suddenly sail right around Australia and head for Africa? Townsend knew he wouldn't get an answer from the radioman. It wasn't just radio silence: it was now avoiding submarines and that worst of all calamities — a Jap Zero who strays overhead and wants to test his 38-caliber guns. They were all over Port Moresby, on the under side of the Solomon Islands. Port Lincoln? What strategic influence was this? But a cargo vessel had to be heading somewhere, and its guns were a poor match for an aircraft coming in at a 45 degree angle. Anything could happen to a defenseless merchantman in the open seas. What a leap of faith Donovan was able to extract from the merchant marine bigwigs in Washington: an around-the-world trip on the maiden voyage of the second ship to come down the ways in Richmond, California?

All the greater reason for hoping Meitner could, as he out it, change Hitler's mind. So he busied himself in the kitchen of the American embassy. The two women preparing caviar for the reception ignored him. They had been told long ago to stay away from any unusual visitors to the kitchen — and this description fit Townsend exactly. For his part, Townsend had little interest in women, no matter what their age, at the moment, no matter how ripe they appeared.

He was dozing in a chair among boxes of produce, bread, and canned fish, his drink held as if in a dead man's hand, when a voice woke him. "Good to see you again, Mister... what is it?..."

"Townsend. Wonderful to see you!" As he scrambled to his feet he offered his guest a drink, knowing she would decline.

"What do the Americans serve the help?" she asked.

"I think this is aquavit," he answered.

"Try me!"

My goodness, Townsend thought. The place must be thoroughly secure. He fixed a drink, complete with the ice he had delivered earlier, and spread his notebook before her. He had never realized this wisp of a woman, perhaps three times his age, could show any humor, any humanity. But here she was, the scientist who had first been able to show that uranium could be made to fission into lower elements, sipping a drink with him as he sat on a carton of cabbage.

"I have this idea," he said cautiously, "that we might be able to spread the rumor that fission won't be able to produce enough energy to make a bomb. That's it. That's why I'm here."

"Good idea, Only about two years too late."

"Why so?"

"You want to get this rumor to the top, right? To Hitler?"

"You're way ahead of me."

"But he's already got Heisenberg working on it."

"He can shut Heisenberg down in a minute."

"On what basis? A rumor?"

"A paper. A new discovery. A calculation...."

"From me?!"

"From any source you can tap."

Lise Meitner thought for a minute. "At least I got a drink out of this. Would you mind pouring another? It's worth a try, but it's not going to happen overnight. I don't have any scientific credibility in Stockholm. I think you'd have to get someone like Einstein to say it won't work."

Townsend brightened. "Would you be willing to ask him to do this?"

"I already have."

THIRTY-THREE

September 2, 1942, Durban, South Africa

The crew from *Hopkins* had been chastened by one of the fiercest storms in the history of the Indian Ocean. The five thousand four hundred or more miles from Port Lincoln, Australia to the East Coast of Africa had taken more than a month. And for what? the crew wondered. It was tough going in the best of weather, at 11 or 12 knots. But in the hurricane-like storms of this strange season Captain Buck had to slow to less than 5 to keep from capsizing under heavy swells. Radio operator Hewey was at his post for eighteen hours a day to keep in touch with ports along the way. The least of the worries of the Captain were Japanese submarines or gunboats. Only a glutton for punishment would brave these seas.

Their hold had ballast of Australian wheat, supposedly needed in South Africa. But even the engine room personnel knew that this wasn't the mission of the U.S. merchant marine. And the U.S. armed guards on board? What in the devil was their contribution to the war effort?

Captain Buck called for general assembly, on deck, when *Hopkins* finally was in safe waters in the humid, smoke-filled harbor of Durban. Maybe the 'Cap'n' can tell us what this is all about, the crew groused.

"Gentlemen, I owe you an explanation," Captain Buck offered with a broad smile.

After what they had gone through, everyone from the gun crews to the stevedores could smile back. Hewey had to contain a wisecrack. O'Hara sat next to him on a hatch cover, which had been badly split in the storm. He wanted to ask if a mail pouch would be waiting for them here, a good month after the last one in Melbourne. The kitchen crew wondered how they could fake another 'spam salad' or 'chicken over rice rice.' This ship wasn't meant for extended periods without refrigeration or re-supply.

"You have every right to wonder what in hell's going on. I'll make it simple. All I know is that we're under orders from Washington. From MARAD. They had a reason for us to deliver the aircraft to Bora Bora. Then they had a reason for us to go further on to New Zealand and Australia. By the way, it had nothing to do with Guadalcanal. The marines have secured a base there. We weren't needed. Maybe they thought we might be backup. But they moved in fast and did the job."

O'Hara wrestled with this 'double speak,' as the gang at home had always called the lingo of the politicians. "Captain Buck, may I ask something?"

"Of course, Mister O'Hara. But first let me finish. We've got a job to do here in Durban. We've got to fix the ship."

"But — if we hadn't come here, we wouldn't have had all that damage to the ship. We wouldn't have had to fix anything."

There was a chorus of grunts of agreement from the crew.

"We were the second ship down the line at Kaiser," the Captain said. "Maybe they were testing us. Testing the welds, to be more to the point."

Hewey nudged O'Hara in the ribs. He whispered, "Ask him if there wasn't a better way to test the ship than trying to sink it."

"You're saying we went more than five thousand miles to see if some welds held up?"

"That was one consideration. Gentlemen, you'll have to trust me on this. Our orders were to get to this port. What happens after that, I don't know."

"Are we gonna unload the wheat?" a voice asked from the forward gun station.

"Good question," the Captain answered. "One thing I *do* know. It's time for shore leave. You heard me before — hear it again. Behave yourselves out there. You've earned it. Now don't lose it. And — by the way — we hope to have mail delivery within a few days. OK?"

Hewey looked at O'Hara with a well-known scowl. He didn't have to say a thing. The scuttlebutt was true. Something weird was going on.

The women in Durban looking for a 'good time' crowded the docks. The war here seemed far away. In Australia, there was fear: constant talk of the Japanese invading and taking over Port Moresby, on the southern side of Guadalcanal. That was the last Allied defense against an invasion of the continent. If the Japanese could drive Douglas MacArthur out of the Philippines, and into hiding in their country, why wouldn't they pick their targets of opportunity in Australia? In such a climate of fear, having a 'good time' seemed either unworthy of a patriotic country, or vaguely fatalistic.

Radioman Hewey again took engine-room man O'Hara under his wing. "Find yourself a good woman," he advised. "Make sure she's not going to get pregnant. And especially make sure she's not going to fall in love with you. You know, even a prostitute is looking for a way out."

"You're telling a stiff prick to have a conscience?"

"I'm telling you to remember what your gal Sue wrote to you." As they lined up to leave the ship, Hewey gave a broad wave of his hand to Captain Buck, patiently watching over the scene. Then he held up a paper, folded it carefully, and stuffed it in his shirt pocket. The Captain nodded. O'Hara thought little of this exchange. The guys who run the ship know what they're doing, that's for sure, he told himself.

Women were plentiful along the docks, but the bars in Durban were fueled by the worst of the trade in the Indian Ocean. This was one place where American sailors weren't coddled. They were the competition, along with the Brits. They fed the monkey, as the expression went. They took the best women, they ate the best food, they bought real booze when everybody else drank rotgut.

"Let's get out of here," O'Hara said after five minutes into a warm beer.

"I'm with you on that, pal. I've got an idea."

"Yeah?"

"There's a guy I want you to meet."

"Not a woman?"

Hewey brightened. So you're thinking along with me, he thought. He looked at the women lining the low benches of the room, supposedly waiting for a dance or a free beer for a few hugs. He waved to a tall, bronze-colored woman whose full legs were crossed widely under a thin skirt. She tossed her blouse open at the front and flashed a thin smile, pointing at herself as if to feign surprise at her selection. He nodded. When she reached the table she nodded to O'Hara and pulled herself as close to him as her broad hips would allow.

Hewey wet his lips with a mischievous grin. "Dolly here is a woman who likes to be whipped," he said matter-of-factly.

"Dolly?" O'Hara questioned.

"Me Dolly," she agreed. She spread her arms behind her neck and shook her breasts defiantly toward Hewey. O'Hara could not fail to notice her nipples pressing against her blouse.

"Those thin German whores keep a whip next to their beds, it's so hard to get them hot otherwise," Hewey explained. "So down here they just accept that us Northeners like to whip 'em. Even if we don't..."

O'Hara nodded. "But I'm...."

"Come on, kid, let's do the gal a favor. She might even teach you something your gal will appreciate—"

"Shut up!"

"Edwin, respect the woman!"

Dolly ended the debate by encircling O'Hara's torso with her more formidable one and kissing him warmly on his forehead. She held him in a tight grip, rubbing her breasts against him. "Beautiful boy," she said, "Warm me up!"

O'Hara raised his face to hers and smiled. "You are a beautiful woman," he said gallantly. "You are too much for me!"

"Now yer talkin,'" Hewey said. "But please, let her take you to the back room." He handed a roll of dollars to the ubiquitous Dolly and feigned pushing them away. O'Hara grinned sheepishly as Dolly led him away.

Twenty minutes later, the two buddies, one in his mid-forties and the other still a teenager, made their way along the docks until they came to a main street. After a few blocks there were trees in front of houses and then a marketplace, on a square that also contained a Victorian hotel. The radioman clapped his young friend on the back. This is it, he said, as if he had just discovered a rare coin.

There was a parlor off the lobby of the hotel, but no bar. The two men sat down. "May I help you?" a man in a turban asked as he entered from an open door. He wore a white suit, punctuated only with a bank of medals over his left pocket.

"Who are you?" O'Hara asked, scarcely looking up.

"I'm with the hotel…"

"Actually, he's the friend I want you to meet," Hewey said.

"Scotch?" the man asked of O'Hara.

"Beer."

"You better have scotch," the stranger said. "I have no beer."

O'Hara expected every bit of this from his friend. Always a mystery. Nothing in life without confusion. Or, as he was wont to say, 'in confusion there's profit.' So he went him one more. "On the rocks?"

"Neat."

That was it. The three men sat around a low table and sipped scotch from small tumblers, without ice. "We're getting the new gun aboard tomorrow," the stranger said. "I hear there was some damage."

"It's been properly logged into the record. There was, in fact, a storm that threw everything halfway loose overboard."

"Good!"

"And you said you had something else. To bring on board."

"Is this young man privy to all this?" the stranger asked, nodding to O'Hara.

O'Hara laughed and threw back a shot of scotch. "I'm privy to mystery. What in hell is going on?"

"OK, I'm bringing some equipment on board. It can locate objects at a distance. It sends out a signal, which bounces off and comes back. I'll have to run it. Very experimental. The Brits hope to install it in their Spitfires."

"My God, man," Hewey said. "You weren't kidding."

"A radio man like you should have invented this long ago. Only it took a bunch of American scientists in Tuxedo Park to do it. You know where Tuxedo Park is."

"Up the Hudson."

"Right."

"What's it called?"

"That comes later. First I want to know if the Captain is ready to load the new gun on board."

"Of course he is. I've told him you were providing it. It will fit the present gun mount, right?"

"Sure. Standard. But I will have to come on board."

"For the gun or the new gadget?"

"The new gadget. Just list me as a mysterious stranger, or a soldier of fortune."

O'Hara felt left out of the game in this ping pong conversation — especially with a man only a few years older than he was. "What's the name of the 'soldier of fortune'?" he asked.

"Oh, that. Townsend. George Townsend."

"And what's the name of this new gadget?"

"Radar."

THIRTY-FOUR

September 15, 1942, Richmond, California

The letter opened up more questions than it answered. The envelope itself was white-washed, so to speak, of any postal information. Maria realized that the Navy censor had to hide sensitive information. But this was strange. No indication of where the letter came from, no date, only her name and the bay she worked in at the shipyard. Then the letter itself: just a few sentences remained on three pages of handwriting. "Don't worry, Mom, I'm safe.... we've come a long way.... we're doing our job of delivering equipment.... Hard to predict when we're returning.... The captain is a great teacher.... I met some other very smart guys, too.... Keep on building these ships as well as you did this one! Love, Edwin."

The first rain of fall—or the last one of summer, depending on one's backward or forward point of view—was falling lightly on the Bay. It was 10 P.M., lunch break on the swing shift. The lights of San Francisco were a canopy against a starless sky. No more blackouts, no more wardens with their pipsqueak whistles. The fear that had driven Japanese Americans off to detention camps was already a thing of the past, but who could bring them back? The war was "over there," not in our backyard. People were drinking again in bars along Market Street and at the 'Top of the Mark.' The Mark Hopkins Hotel and the Fairmount were the favored "goodbye, we'll be home again before you know it" farewell locations for all the young men shipping out to the far Pacific. There was that word again, Maria thought: *Hopkins.*

Slowly the rain built, sweeping in through the Golden Gate, now in torrents as the women of Bay Three went back to work for the final three hours of their shift. The graveyard crew would drifting in early tonight, perhaps well before their 1 A.M. starting time, because the boss was scheduled to announce a new pay schedule—maybe in person. It was the mid-month adjustment. The yard had met and exceeded their performance schedule. "Liberty ships" were now coming off the line in three weeks, from laying of the keel to sliding down the ways. Mr. Kaiser had something to do with that, but so did the 'muscle builders,' as he liked to call them. Maria was in fact proud of how her arms had bulked up from swinging a welding torch seven hours a day.

At the stroke of midnight, Henry J. Kaiser strode into the rec room of the main yard and walked straight to a microphone at its small stage. This was where an occasional dance was held, an amateur play was put on, or even a Laurel and Hardy movie played. The plant whistle bleated, and soon the room was crowded with workers happy to take an unexpected break.

"Ladies and gents, wonderful friends all—the eagle has shit once again!" the boss crowed. One thing Henry had learned long ago—don't be afraid to talk the same language as you're going to hear behind your back. The audience loved it. The boss was one of them!

Once the laughter had subsided, he continued, "The guys who write the checks have given us all a raise. The incentive worked! We've now got 32 ships in action. Imagine how long it took to get that first one! Then the second. Some of those ships have carried their cargo out to our boys in the Pacific, and are coming back already for their second trips! Even third trips! That's the way we're gonna win this war!"

Maria nudged her comrade in arms, her Japanese friend whose family had been relocated—as they put it kindly—to some place in Utah or Nevada—she didn't know which. Maria raised her hand like a fourth-grader eager to give an answer. The boss didn't see her. He was intent on something else.

"So your paycheck, starting this week, is going up three dollars a day. How does that sound?"

The crowd loved it. The few men on hand whistled. Some women screamed their approval. Mr. Kaiser had them in the palm of his hand, as usual. Maria decided to walk up to the stage, even though jostled on all sides.

"Mister Kaiser!" she called out. "I have a question." She caught his eye.

Henry always hoped for reaction from his workers. He had learned this lesson all the way from paving roads in Oregon to building the Grand Coulee Dam. This was no exception. Best of all, this was a woman who had called him out once before. "Mrs. O'Hara, am I right?"

"Yeah, that's me. Just a little question."

"Let's have it."

"What was the name of the second ship that came down this line?"

Henry Kaiser stood speechless for a moment, then turned to an aide for help. "This is a test, right?" he quipped.

"Oh, I know the answer, all right. I worked on it. Best of all, my son's on it."

"Mrs. O'Hara, now I see why you're asking. Tell us the name, please."

"It's the *Stephen Hopkins*. You know, like the Mark Hopkins in Ess Eff."

"Got it. Where is it now?"

"That's just it, Mr. Kaiser. I get letters from my son, but they've blacked out all that information. That ship of yours hasn't come back yet, from the Pacific."

Henry Kaiser's face suddenly turned somber. This was not the time to joke around. He had yet to receive a report from the Maritime Administration of any of his ships being sunk, or even fired upon. He stepped down off the stage and approached Maria O'Hara. "I didn't mean to—"

"Mr. Kaiser, you're a perfect gentleman. You haven't done anything wrong. I'm just wondering what's happening."

"Sure. But I don't know—"

"You don't and I don't."

"I'll try to find out."

"Please...."

187

THIRTY-FIVE

September 22, 1942, Libreville, French Equatorial Africa

The German raider anchored a mile off shore while the supply ship *Tannenfels* was winched as close as possible to the long dock of the port. It was unseasonably hot weather, but the crew liked it: the heavy humidity spilled bursts of rain all along the coast, clearing the mosquitoes and breaking up the drudgery of loading truckload after truckload of sulfurous ore into the hold of the ship.

Horst Gerlach knew his vessel, *Stier*, would have to double as a merchantman on this voyage — even though it was outfitted for nothing but combat. Before the war *Stier* was hardly a bull, as the name proclaimed: it was the German version of a luxury liner. It plied the icy waters of the North Sea with German tourists on holiday. Unlike *Bremen* and her sister ships that carried Americans to the Olympic Games in Berlin in 1936, *Stier* was built for speed and ice-breaking. These characteristics made her an ideal conversion into a "raider," otherwise known to her enemies as a Q-boat — an unknown quantity. She had wide staterooms on her second deck, whose walls, on command, fell forward on tracks to reveal 5.9" cannons on either side. Accordingly, she flew two sets of flags, one benignly Germanic and the other fiercely Nazi.

Commander Gerlach winced as his crew methodically off-loaded crates of shells and even spare cannons onto barges to be taken ashore for storage. Every bit of cargo space on his ship was needed for this strange sort of ore that had to be mined in the heart of Africa. These were orders: between them, *Stier* and *Tannenfels* had to deliver an enormous load of rock to Hamburg. His intelligence officer informed him it was an advanced metallic element known as uranium, but as far as he was concerned it might as well have been called Lusitanium or, for that matter, "What's that other planet? Plutonium."

"You'll have plenty of ballast, this time," his chief engineer joked. "They'll never mistake you for a cruise ship."

The captain was fond of working with large charts, both for navigation and for timelines. He had been a mathematics student before he had to find work in the rebuilding of the German Navy. Admiral Doenitz inspired him to use his first love to improve his naval performance. True, he would never make admiral, and his ship was expendable, but he would do his duty for the fatherland. Gerlach therefore studiously lined the walls of his stateroom with large travel posters, pinned up with tacks—only they were turned backwards to present a "tabula rasa" of large white space. He drew heavy lines down the left side of each and across the bottom: perfect x,y coordinates. If he was presenting a time schedule, he would mark off the hours across the bottom, and then the goal to be accomplished up the left side.

He called his staff into his stateroom for a briefing. "As you can see," he said professorially, "we have 96 hours to load 250 tons of rock. Clear?" Everyone nodded, knowing that they were allowed to smile only when he broke the first smile. "So—here we are," he announced, pointing at the lower left-hand corner of the chart. "No rock, no time elapsed. Clear?"

A young officer raised his hand and was acknowledged. "But the clock is now running and we are not loading any rock."

"Ah! Very good. So our line is going to run across the bottom of the table, as the clock ticks, and will begin to rise only when we move into the wharf and begin loading. Ja?"

What else is new? the look on the staff's faces said.

"All right, all right—just my little game, you might say," Gerlach recognized. "But such things have a tendency to get complicated. And that's when it pays to have some idea of time versus accomplishment." He suddenly became stern. "My intelligence officer has informed me we are crucial to the war effort. This is not a game. What we are loading is going to create a new kind of bomb."

The captain could just as well dropped a bomb on his heavy carpet. "Yes, gentlemen, I am told it will be the bomb that will win the war. I am allowed to reveal this to you, because you must do your duty to the fullest. If you do not, if we do not deliver this cargo on time...." Gerlach walked backed to his desk and removed a large marker from a drawer. He returned to his chart and slashed a red scar across the entire page. "Then we are dead as a country, we will face starvation and devastation worse than we did after the first war. Do you understand?"

The room was silent. The officers had never seen their captain in a state like this. He had taken them to bars, even to brothels. Theirs was a dangerous mission, and he realized there had to be compensation or there would be rebellion. Or at least dereliction of duty. It was the old story of a carrot or a stick. He believed in the carrot.

Gerlach returned to his desk and pulled a bottle of shlibovitz from the bottom drawer. "Are any of you Hungarians?" he asked rhetorically, as he had asked on many an occasion. He scattered a handful of shot glasses across the desk. "Shall we drink to a successful trip?"

Two bottles later, Gerlach was satisfied he had done the right thing. But he had one further lesson to pass on. He pointed out the window at the barges going ashore with his stock of shells and equipment. "We're lightening up our armament to get more rocks on board. Stupid, right? How're we going to explain this to the crew?"

"General assembly —" a young officer blurted out.

"Anyone else? Ordinarily, I'd agree with our brash youth. But I'm a practical man. I think they already know something fishy's going on. Why would be so interested in this ore shipment? A lot of these guys were down here before, when we explored the area. They know it's not just iron ore. But maybe they think it's aluminum, for airplanes. Or copper, for shells. Maybe they don't give a shit. So, what would I recommend?"

"Keep it quiet," one man said.

"Exactly. In war, gentlemen, they really don't give a shit. And remember, we've got about four hundred men out there, each one of them a potential trouble-maker."

"So what do we tell 'em, after staggering out of here with a buzz on?"

"Tell 'em it's top secret. But when we come back here to pick up our ammo, we're going to have one helluva party, with all the Frenchies in town and a woman for every man."

"Captain, we've told 'em this so many times...."

"Tell 'em again!"

THIRTY-SIX

September 23, 1942, Capetown, South Africa

Captain Paul Buck felt a twinge of nostalgia as he signed papers in the port at Capetown, as he had done for many years in the major ports of South America as a captain for the United Fruit Corporation. This time he was carrying no cargo—yet he was on a journey so wildly different from transporting bananas that he easily believed he had entered another world. Like every captain, he had to disassociate his own interests from the lives of his crew. He now found that exercise very hard.

His chief engineer, Rudy Rutz, had a wife and newborn daughter when he left the cruise ship business to sign on with *Hopkins*. Rudy was a wiry fellow with many ambitions. At the moment, the sea was his way of making a living for his family. Charlie Fitzgerald and George Cronk completed the engineering team under Rutz. Between them they were frequently looking for a fourth for bridge, a way of whiling away the time on long seagoing journeys. None of them felt like a card game at the moment. Captain Buck had made it clear this was their last stop in a real port for some time to come. He hadn't made it clear where they were headed. What in the devil was out there in the South Atlantic, or in South America, or in the horn of Africa, for that matter? And why would this single ship be looking for any particular kind of cargo in any of these locations?

The radioman, Hewey, wasn't very helpful. He might tell you what was happening, but not what was coming up. So the engineers decided to put the question to the captain—just as soon as all the paperwork was taken care of. The crew was admittedly a thin one, just about 40 guys. So it should be easy to go to each of them, and put a big brother arm around a shoulder, and tell the guy the Maritime Administration often has plans of its own, and can't share 'em with everybody in the service. And yet.... If the captain would come clean, and give them some kind of lowdown on what's happening, it would be so much easier to put everyone's mind at ease.

Suddenly there was a long, low well-known sound — the rifling of a shell from a gun, screeching off into the ocean, instantaneously, it seemed, followed by the blast of an explosive. What in hell!?

It soon became apparent that Captain Buck had wasted no time to test his new gun mount, on the aft deck. Two men took shells from a long, wooden case and fed them from one to the other to the loading carriage of a cannon. A third man discharged the previous shell casing and cleared the breech for reloading. Several hundred yards off shore, a bright flag signaled a target mounted on a buoy. A plume of water shot into the air as the first round plunged into the ocean, a half mile away. The targeted buoy bounced up brightly in the water, clearly under the spray from the shot. The three men working the gun, the contingent of the 'Armed Guards' assigned to the merchant marine by the Navy, showed for the first time on this voyage that they had some specific duties to perform other than manning the machine gun buckets.

Engineers Rutz, Cronk, and Fitzgerald watched the exhibition with a mixture of pride and confusion. What in the devil was so important that there was special target practice, for some kind of a special cannon, in this god-forsaken, crassly commercial port at the tip of South Africa? The war was three thousand miles away to the East, two thousand miles away to the north, and home was twenty-five hundred miles to the West. Were these the kind of calculations that tourists are accustomed to make as they spin around the globe on an around-the-world adventure?

The engineers found Captain Buck in a jovial mood. He seemed in little hurry to announce their next port of call. "May I invite you up top for a gin and tonic?" he said with unusual nonchalance. "That's the favored drink down here, you know, with all the Brits in charge."

Another blast from below and a whistle of a shell punctuated the afternoon. The captain shrugged and smiled. "Target practice...."

The four men settled into deck chairs on the second cabin level. A bottle of Beefeaters and a pitcher of tonic water in an ice bucket were in the middle of the table. "Let me get some more glasses," Captain Buck said; "I was expecting only ....our visitor."

Before the captain returned, George Townsend made his way up the stairs and introduced himself to the ship's engineers. It was unseasonally warm: at this time of the year, early winter winds could be expected. The four men traded chit chat, uncomfortably. The "visitor," as he had become known to the crew, knew 'more than he let on,' as everybody agreed. But on one matter they had something to discuss openly. What was this new thing, radar?

Townsend had regaled everyone with his years at the University of California, his brush with physicists, his love of adventure. But did he have a reason for, out of nowhere, becoming part of the crew? After the first sip of gin and tonic, all round, with Captain Buck settled comfortably in his "captain's chair," Townsend felt it was time for some candor.

"I don't know any more than you do, guys," he began, "but somebody upstairs asked me to test this gizmo out."

Captain Buck raised his usual caution. "It's top secret, you know. And this time I'm not joking. The Germans don't have it, the Japs don't have it, and the best thing is they don't have any fucking idea that WE have it.'

"I don't have to tell you," Townsend added, "that there are Japs and Krauts roaming all over this place. So just tell anybody you talk to that this's just another radio antenna. OK?"

"Better yet," Buck said, "nobody goes ashore!"

Rutz and Fitzgerald looked at each other with mild astonishment. "Another day without women, eh Cap?"

"You can't afford 'em," Buck answered.

"Ah ha! But we do have some fun ahead," Townsend said. "Can I tell 'em?"

Rutz had been on merchantmen too long to believe in fairy tales. "You guys had some kinda lovin' in Durban, as I remember," he added. You tell me you're gonna top this?"

Captain Buck poured himself another drink and raised his glass. "Here's to the good things in life!"

"Boo!"

"Listen, gang. We're going to have good liquor, good food, and plenty of R&R after we get to Brazil."

"Brazil!?"

"If all goes well, that's our first stop heading home."

The engineers clinked their glasses with Townsend. Then an idea spread over Rutz's face. "So, hotshot, is this why we need this radio thing? To navigate to Brazil?"

Townsend looked at the captain, and Buck nodded. "Not exactly," he said. "Let me tell you how it works. Cause you guys're going to have to *work* it."

"Shouldn't we get Hewey in on this?" Rutz asked.

"Already have."

"Then shoot."

George Townsend thought back in a flash about what had brought him here: his chance meeting with some 'older' women in a bar in Manhattan, his quick trip to Washington, his signing on with a wild man named Donovan, who worked for the President of the United States but out of his office in Rockefeller Center, his indoctrination with another wild man, Robert Oppenheimer, out in the mesas of New Mexico, his trips to a beautiful, truly 'older' woman in Stockholm, who had invented, if that's the word, the disintegration of a big fat element into other parts, also known as the fission of uranium, his escapades with the clumsy Gestapo and not-so-clumsy SS, his scouting of German ships in a harbor in French Guinea, like a baseball scout looking for prospects at shortstop, his 'seance' in Tuxedo Park with the inventors of a strange new weapon, and, best of all, his order from the wild

Irish man at OSS: 'just do it, kid.' So he thought for a brief moment. What did he have to say, rather than tell? Ah, that's the difference. Just say. So he did.

"This is a tool that sends radio signals out there, hits things, and then, as the radio signals bounce back, listens to them."

"So then if we read the signals..."

"Right! We know where they came from and so what they bounced off of."

"But...."

"Right, but. How do we read them? That's the baby! On a screen. Radio signals reduced to a screen."

Captain Buck shook his head from side to side, as if to say, what'll they think of next? He may as well said it. "Do the Germans know anything about this?"

Townsend winked at Hewey. "Last night me and a couple of your, er, staff, tried to find out. We decided to get some suspicious looking Krauts drunk."

"Krauts?"

"They're all over the place. Especially the brothels. They think they can hold their liquor better than anybody on the planet. And they fuck and run! So they think they have an edge on us."

"And you—"

"We fuck lovingly and longly. We listen to the squeals in the room next door. You know our secret?"

Captain Buck grinned blankly like a straight man.

"Our secret is we drink while we screw. Sometimes the girls have to help us out. And you know something?"

"What?"

"They love it! All of 'em say it: it makes us seem like amateurs. The most hellish whore in the world wants to think she's helping."

Captain Buck had to shake his head. "So now you've written the philosophy of the whorehouse. What's that got to do—"

"The bloody Germans were putting their pants on before we began to slap ass. We could hear 'em talking in the parlor. Get this: they suspect we're up to something. They mentioned Tannenfels twenty times if they said it once. But they can't believe our Hopkins is anything but a supply ship."

"Who else was there with you?"

"Bunch of guys. Hewey, the radioman. I think guys from the engine room."

"Hewey's clued in on this radar gizmo, right?"

"We had plenty of time to go over it in Durban, too."

Rutz wasn't satisfied. "So you brought this toy all the way down here, just so we could have a nice safe trip across the Atlantic?"

"Where did I say that?" Townsend laughed.

"We've got a crew down here, Captain, that's just as antsy as we are about what's going down. What do we tell 'em?"

"Tell 'em to do their job and shut up."

"But they keep asking..."

"Tell 'em again!"

THIRTY-SEVEN

September 27, 1942, South Atlantic

Three hours outbound from Capetown, Captain Buck had called a general assembly to explain to all hands the purpose and destination of the voyage into an ocean they had never imagined, on beginning this trip, that they would ever see. Their written orders, he told them, were to take on a load of bauxite in French Guinea. That meant climbing up the West African coast into the "horn" of the continent. Yes, a strange place to settle on as a destination and as a cargo of all the multitude of places and cargoes one could easily imagine. He explained that as a captain he took orders from his bosses just as he expected them to take orders from him. Without having to know all the details, without understanding the risks, without being aware even of the destination. This was the only way things can work in a wartime situation, he said: "Ours not to reason why...." He didn't have to finish the quote, and he wished he had something a little less stale to tell them.

Yet! He also had something good to report. An important date would be coming up in two days: Thanksgiving! Maybe it was celebrated in the states in November, and probably on the fourth Thursday, as President Roosevelt had urged. But they had been away from home so long—since April!—that the Captain thought it might be a nice idea to have a holiday. And on a Sunday, when most of the crew expected a day off, anyway. So they had loaded turkeys aboard in Capetown, and the mess crew would be working up a full dinner for everybody. So save your appetite, he advised: on the 27th we should have one big celebration. It would be a little touch of home even out in a vast area of the South Atlantic, where not much else seemed to be happening, and where only the slavers of the last three centuries, who plied the grim trade that would leave scars on the world for centuries more, had made any mark on history.

Thanksgiving, indeed, Townsend thought, in the pre-dawn hours of Sunday, September 27. What better way to celebrate an attack on a German naval vessel, what better way to calm everyone's nerves on 'game day.' Yes, it might just turn out this way, he told his radioman, Hewey.

They had converted a drafting board and a plotting table into a jerry-rigged radar station. To a small round dial, somewhat larger than a temperature gauge but unlike anything Hewey had ever seen, wires ran across the floor and out the observation window to the ship's central mastheads. There, like some sort of a metallic windsock, a device rotated slowly over 360 degrees. Evening squalls had intensified after midnight, and now the decks were being lashed with cascades of rain. Visibility was reduced to about a quarter mile, not bad considering the peas-soup fogs they had seen in California and, much later, in the South China Sea and Indian Ocean.

Radioman Hewey peered into the oval screen before him, like a psychic into a crystal ball. The overhead light was dimmed to the point of eeriness. "What in hell'm I looking for?" he asked. "I see the magic wand spiraling around. It's like a clock hand running too fast. That's the deal, right?"

"You got it. It's in sync with the locator up top."

"The locator, huh?"

"That's what I call it. The guys in the back room no doubt have a damn fine name for it."

"All I see is rain."

"That's all that's there right now."

"So the spinner keeps going around and it's sending radio signals out in all directions of the compass..."

"And when it hits something solid—"

"Like the ship next to us in Capetown—"

"Right. A big blob."

"Bring me a coffee, will you? That is, if you want me to stay awake —"

"You, sir, we got all the coffee you need. It's now five bells. I say we're within a few hours of our targets...."

This was one morning when dawn didn't come up like thunder. It was black out there, everyone on the bridge agreed. This didn't stop Captain Buck from arriving in the wheelhouse at precisely seven. The engineers kidded him that the only clock he needed was the sound of the screw. The morning watch, Paul Porter, still had an hour of lookout before he took to his bunk. He commented to the Captain that the ship's position didn't seem to have any danger, as they were not really hugging the coast. "That's right," Buck answered, but said no more.

"Shall I read out our position, captain?" Porter asked.

"Check it when you go off."

Townsend quietly opened the door of the wheelhouse with a draft of wind and rain following him. "Maybe an announcement at nine?" he asked.

"Let's do it at eight. Just a reminder: turkey and all the trimmings at Noon — so spare yourself breakfast —"

"Something like that."

"No news, eh?"

"Just that our targets left Libreville 16 hours ago. Typical Germans. Right after lunch —"

"Germans?" Porter asked incredulously. "What's with —"

"They're all over the fuckin' place. I mean, no cause for alarm. Just have to watch out for the enemy. And we left the Japs behind way back there...." Townsend smiled at the watch officer, a good ten years his senior, as if to say, I guess I'm not going to bullshit you.

"Whatever you say," Porter conceded. "I'm hittin' the sack."

It was half past seven, and Hewey was fast losing his night vision following the sweep of the "clock hand" around the dial on top of his plotting table. Captain Buck had given his crew his advice about saving their appetite for lunch. The

201

mess was half full for breakfast. "May I spell you?" Townsend asked as he came back to the radio room. "Why don't you go over and shoot the shit with the captain?"

Hewey picked up his third coffee of the morning, opened the radio room door, and emptied the cup unceremoniously onto the deck. "One thing you'd think the mess could do," he said, "is make a decent coffee." Townsend sat down at the plotting table and glanced at the small oval screen. He cupped his hands over his temples, as the blackness of five o'clock had now turned into the grayness of coming up on nine.

"Don't leave!" he said. "See if you see what I see."

Hewey looked over Townsend's shoulder. "Got it. A couple stars just showed up."

"You bet. Now plot the damn things. I'll time you."

"Two objects north northeast.... Closing."

"Eight forty-five—"

"Closing..."

"Jesus Christ! Tell the captain fast starboard!"

Captain Paul Buck sounded General Quarters—the command to man the battle stations. He had never faced an enemy ship in battle. Yet he understood one thing from hours of target practice: it usually takes two shots, over and under, to get the range. And if you aim your ship right at the enemy you can avoid a lot of that kind of "over and under." It was how he understood avoiding torpedoes: don't present a broadside target. His Liberty ship, *Hopkins*, was sailing in ballast—no cargo, riding high in the water. That was a double reason to face the enemy head on. He checked his bearing. It was 24 44 South, 21 50 West. The 'black gang' in the engine room knew instantly something was up. This is no exercise, Chief Rudy Rutz yelled: pile on the boilers. Orders for ramping up the engines blasted over the intercom as if to answer Rutz.

Down in the engine room, the black gang heard sporadic bursts of machine gun fire that told Edwin O'Hara that his 'big brother' Ensign Kenneth Willett had swung his crew into action. The Naval Armed Guards were getting the range first.

Word was passed down that two German ships were closing fast, but neither had been hit. Could anybody see anything?

Seconds went by like minutes. What was happening upstairs? The silence was heavy as the gang stared at each other in the full knowledge that at any moment a torpedo or an explosion from a cannon could pierce the steel walls that stood between them and the ocean. And then there was the magazine—the stores of shells that could ignite like a hundred bombs.

"Upstairs" on the bridge, Captain Buck and 'adventurer' Townsend put aside their glasses and strained to see what was coming at them through the fog, even as their gunners fired at shadows. Suddenly there was a break in the squall line: Lookouts yelled over the intercom: Mayday! Mayday!

Buck, Hewey, and Townsend spied a bulbous, lumbering vessel coursing toward them, spouting fire and belches of black smoke. As events would show later, first in line was *Stier*, a 'raider' converted from a travel ship into a Q-boat—a lion in lamb's clothing. Behind it, almost in formation, was a larger merchantman, *Tannenfels*. The raider hadn't been looking for trouble, but there it was right ahead of it. With a crew of almost 400, and six-inch guns fore and aft, *Stier* swung into action like a marching band.

Three shots rifled toward *Hopkins* before the gun crew of the Liberty ship could bring its aft 6-inch gun around for a counter punch. Ensign Willett, one of the first Naval Armed Guards to board a merchantman, was in charge of the *Hopkins* gun crews, and as he raced to the 50-caliber rifle tubs himself to get some rounds off a blast of shrapnel cut through him from the first hit. He staggered over his gun and began firing aimlessly at the fast approaching German ships.

Despite the American ship's advantage in "seeing" the enemy first and spraying shells through the squall, the firepower of the German ships soon began to take their toll. The first exchange from gunnery crews on either side was a fireworks display: they both found their range quickly.

The blast that felled Willett crashed through the upper decks amidships, kicked up explosions, and penetrated down to the starboard engine room. Lights went out and a boiler burst, spraying hissing steam everywhere. O'Hara snapped on his battle lantern to see First Engineer Fitzgerald crumpled under a mass of twisted steel. Chief Rutz screamed in pain from scalding of his upper body, then yelled to his crew to grab the wounded and pull them forward, out of the acrid fumes that were engulfing the engine room.

Only O'Hara and fellow 'black gang' man George Cronk were unscathed. With Rutz they went back into the engine room as far as the sulfurous smoke would allow them, to try to reach more of the wounded. They were forced back to the ballast-free holds where at least they could see ahead of them.

Hopkins was now without power.

Machine gun fire raked the upper deck and smashed Captain Buck's left shoulder. Radioman Hewey clung to his post as Townsend hit the deck. But Captain Buck was not yet done: he knew his gunnery crews were still firing. Their first direct hit came from the wild spraying of Willett's 50-caliber gun, and it was a lucky break — the only one they would have that day.

Stiers' diesel generator broke into flames and electrical power flashed off. The ship's ammunition hoists were locked in train, leaving her gun crews empty-handed. *Tannenfels* was unhappily positioned behind smoke rising from *Spier,* and was hit with cannon fire at the waterline.

Almost at the same time, a fourth round of 6-inch shells from *Stier* again careened into the deckhouse of *Hopkins* and sent shrapnel across the deck, killing Willett. Captain Buck was again hit, but continued to maneuver by steering the ship by himself to gain a better angle for his main gun. That was the only hope of taking an enemy ship down with him.

But Willett's crew was scattered — their shell boxes were open, ready for reloading, but little could be done to mount a counterattack as explosions rolled across the deck.

It was an alley fight, a merciless brawl. Hewey and Townsend were finally thrown out of the radio room by a second direct hit of a 6-inch shell. The gun crews on the second level were scorched in the flames that continued to erupt below decks. But they had no safe place to run to—all they could do was to try to return fire. Sulfurous smoke spat up through the holds—those on top could only pity what was happening below decks.

CaptainBuck knew what he had to do. He grabbed his code book and set it ablaze, then ordered his signalman to pull the cord that whistled 'Abandon ship." He would remain on the bridge to take any last shots from his adversary. Buck was still alive as lifeboats #1 and #2 spilled down the port side, and he saw his men scrambling to find their way to the water. Then the Captain disappeared in a final blast from a shell that demolished the bridge.

Still below decks, Rutz and Cronk heard the signal to abandon and made their way to the listing port side. The fumes from burning steel and bodies were overwhelming. O'Hara was set to follow with others of his gang.

Then the nineteen-year-old cadet made a different decision. Why, no one would ever know. It was the kind of decision that comes from another view of life, another sense of battle. Once he fixed on it, he seemed impervious to danger. He climbed through flames on an abandoned ship as if, dreamlike, he was in a different world.

O'Hara apparently had learned that there was a shaft tunnel that ran up to the aft deck by way of an 'escape trunk.' It was folly to try to use this tunnel on a burning ship: from the lifeboats, O'Hara's crewmates could see him and had to believe he was crazy. That's where you got caught and burned to death. A catwalk led to a ladder up to the aft gun platform, and its magazine was right above him, waiting to explode. They watched in horror as the magazine was hit and exploded, hurling O'Hara back to the catwalk, now dangling over water.

But the cadet got up and scaled the ladder once again to the gun platform. There it was right in front of him, the 'special' gun, with its shell box open. He was now focused on one thing only.

As if in slow motion, the dream must have floated before his eyes: The practice rounds he had watched on Treasure Island in San Francisco Bay. The hints he got from Chief Rutz on Bora Bora. The taunting from the mystery man, George Townsend, in Durban. That special gun, brought aboard, something like the Excalibur sword that King Arthur and the Knights of the Round Table had used to vanquish the evil pretenders of old England. Now that gun was in his grasp. The Gun.

O'Hara dug into the ammunition box and muscled a 90-lb. shell up to the Gun. He dropped it into the breech, closed the block, and shouldered the weapon into a direct line at the German attackers. He pulled the lanyard and was hurled backward by a roar of recoil and flash of fire from the muzzle. Before he could clear his ears he saw an explosion erupting from the lead ship.

He pried open a second box next to the Gun. Four more shells! One after another, O'Hara loaded them into the breech, locked down, and fired. The enemy ships were now so close on each other than he couldn't tell which ship he hit. But every shell did. At the very moment he saw what he had done, a roar of 50 caliber machine gun fire killed him instantly.

Stier was now burning as eerily as *Hopkins*. Captain Gerlach gave the abandon ship order as had his adversary. Oh, yes, his gun crews had finally put an end to that man who came out of nowhere to sink them. But Captain Gerlach was still alive. He could not understand what had hit him. But he knew his duty: he ordered the scuttling charges to be set.

Within a half hour of their meeting on that Sunday morning, a morning that had promised a turkey dinner and voyages back to home ports, two ships, German and

American, slipped, burning, into the cold waters of the South Atlantic.

An American captain and his deckhand, years apart in age and training, but close in dedication to duty, went down together.

THIRTY-EIGHT

September 29, 1942, Reich Chancellery, Berlin

The report... what report? Oh, the Heisenberg program. Yes? Admiral Doenitz, speak up! Did I hear you say Heisenberg has given up on it? Yes? If he can't do it, then find somebody who will.... We need that bomb. Do you understand? We need that bomb....

What?! We don't have any place to build it? Impossible! Build it in the Reichstag! They'll never bomb us in Berlin.... All right, they hit the railroad yards. Then build it in Munich! Put Goebbels on the phone.... I mean Goering.... Yes, Herman, for God's sake....

Herman? The rockets are coming along, is that right? Good! Tell me again, who's in charge at Peenemunde. Werner von Braun? Yes, I remember. Bright young man. Good future ahead of him.... Early next year!? I thought he had the fucking rockets on the assembly line! Is he there? Can he come to the phone? Well, where in hell is he? I want him in Berlin tomorrow. Full report.

Herman, I know you're doing your best. If von Braun can get you those jet fighters, they'll never bomb Berlin. Put Doenitz back on.

Admiral, der Fuehrer. I'm losing my patience with the bomb program. You know me well enough to tell me the truth. What is really happening, huh?

Oh. Uh huh. But you say we don't really need the uranium, after all? Did I hear you right? Who changed that idea, Heisenberg? Did he change his mind before or after the ships were sunk? Just tell me straight: before or after? I said, before or after!?

You don't know.... All right, Admiral. Just get the reports from those ships and get back to me. Somebody will hang if I find out.... No, I trust your men, Admiral. The wolf pack is our best weapon. So far. Keep pouring it on. Put Goebbels on.

Joseph! Give me a report on the camps. Those vermin.... Once we get them rooted out we'll win this war. Yes, gas. The quicker the better. None of them are any use to use. They'll sabotage us if we try to work them. I only wish we had the bomb to use on them. The bomb—you know, the Heisenberg project. Why is everybody dodging around this? Yes, we lost a ship bringing the goods here. But they tell me it doesn't matter. Their theory was wrong. Just as long as the Jews in America have a theory that's wrong, too. They do? Why do you say that?

Oh. They didn't try to sink us. And they could have. Yes, I understand. Just an accident at sea....

THIRTY-NINE

October 2, 1942, Richmond, California

Naval personnel were always coming and going in the shipyard. Some of them were high level, some of them inspectors. The women on the morning and the swing shifts saw a lot of them. They had roving eyes, everyone joked. Hadn't they ever seen a busty woman in coveralls before?

But there was one type of Navy man that the women could sense a parking lot away. This guy usually came in a car with a driver. The driver saluted and stood by the car. The guy always carried an envelope. It wasn't an envelope full of checks from Uncle Sam. It was a death notice.

At least a third of the women in the yards had fathers or husbands or brothers or sons in the service. Everyone knew, from the mail calls and the "visits" and the crying afterward, who they were. The war was only ten months old on this October day, but already that dreadful automobile from the Department of War had made its call several dozen times.

Production didn't stop during those impromptu meetings of mothers, sisters, or daughters and the messenger of death. Regulations called for such private notices to be delivered, if at all possible, to the home. But home addresses were hard to come by in these unsettled times. The women who worked the shipyards tended to use the yard as their preferred address. There was nothing untoward about this: the yard was, in fact, a community. Henry Kaiser himself had promoted this idea. What better support group than one's fellow workers, one's place of accomplishment instead of place of loneliness?

It was midweek, a time for rain to fall if it had to, at the end of summer. And on this particular day it had started early and swept into the afternoon. It was Maria's week for the swing shift, the one she liked best. She could head back to her little apartment in Berkeley after Midnight, have a nightcap, and still get in a good night's sleep.

The car arrived in the parking lot at five o'clock, just after Maria's gang was in "full swing on the swing," as they liked to call it. The radio blared out one of the Hit Parade top tens of the month, "Maria Elena say/That we will never part...." Maria O'Hara watched as the officer—it was always an officer—strode forcefully toward the yard office. There, everyone knew, he would find his directions from the employment people, and make his way directly to the shop floor. The production line would stop. After a few words with the shop steward, the officer would look up and down the assembly line, find his person, nod to the steward, and walk to that person. It was a ritual dance of some delicacy. Everyone understood what it meant, and appreciated the civility with which it was carried out.

As the officer approached Maria O'Hara's work station, her closest friend on the line rushed over to her. Everyone on this line knew that Maria hadn't heard from her son in weeks. The officer asked for her by full name, and saluted. "I have the solemn duty and deep regret to inform you that your son Edwin O'Hara, United States Merchant Marine, has been killed in action."

FORTY

October 20, 1942, Recife, Brazil

A sea wall extends from the quiet Portuguese harbor of Recife well into the Atlantic ocean. On an un usually hot Fall afternoon, along this barrier a rudderless, mastless vessel—a lifeboat — washed desolately toward the inner harbor. Sailors from the port threw a line to the ship and pulled it in to a dock. What they saw was terrifying. Fifteen gaunt men, most of them shirtless and shivering from sickness and fatigue, waved up at them with bulging eyes and muttered their thanks through parched lips. They had sailed one thousand eight hundred miles, across the Atlantic. They were the survivors of *Hopkins,* the U.S. merchantman that had sunk the German raider Stier.

News of the battle had already spread around the world. A full three weeks earlier, the *New York Times* printed a page one story of the encounter of the lightly armed U.S. Maritime Administration vessel and the notorious Q-boat. It was wonderful newspaper copy: the Germans and the Japanese seemed to be having their way across the globe, from Java to Stalingrad. U.S. marines were dug in at Guadalcanal, holding on grimly against the relentless attacks of a far superior enemy force. North Africa was in turmoil, with the 'desert fox' Rommel still threatening to make a run at Cairo. So even if this was just the South Atlantic, a U.S. victory—if one could call it that—was good news for the American public.

Four of the *Hopkins* participants of the battle did not survive the lifeboat voyage to Brazil., among them Chief Engineer Rutz. Five of the Armed Guards did make it all the way — most likely because they were among the youngest and best trained on board. They brought back with them confirmation of the heroism of the crew, especially Willett, Buck, and the "teenager" O'Hara.

The newspaper stories were already forgotten as the men recuperated in Recife. But here, at least, they were treated as heroes. It was a port city full of history—and generous people. In the seventeenth century, the city was populated by the Dutch West Indies Company. Unlike its sister trading corporation of Amsterdam, this company was Jewish from top to bottom. Its founders hoped it would be the 'New Jerusalem.' But Portuguese traders soon infiltrated it and, once again, as has happened down through history, expelled its Jewish population. There was one upside: the Jewish settlers went north to what was then New Amsterdam. The Dutch reluctantly allowed these "foreign" settlers into the New World—and into what is now New York City.

The survivors of *Hopkins* reported that the 'mysterious stranger' who boarded in Durban, South Africa, had perished in the battle. There was no one to confirm or deny this report, except for the stranger himself. In fact, George Townsend failed to make the lifeboat. But he did see a chance to mingle with the several hundred German sailors who had to abandon *Stier*. The man who had prowled the streets of Copenhagen and Libreville one step ahead of the SS was now in his element. When he was picked up by a lifeboat from *Tannenfels,* he was wearing only the dungarees of a deck hand. Asked his name, he blurted out the first things that came to mind, the German raider and his alias in Sweden. "Wilhelm Rader," he growled in his best German accent.

Tannenfels returned to Libreville to disgorge its 400 extra passengers. Bill Rader, as he now called himself, lost himself among the French population, found a radio receiver, and reported his exploits to New York. Wild Bill Donovan listened with glee to his account, which differed substantially from that of the *New York Times.*

"I think the secret of radar is safe," Donovan said. "And some day you'll have to tell me about my compatriot, O'Hara!"

Bill Rader, as he was known for the rest of the war, went on to serve in Croatia, Italy, the South of France, and eventually lost a good part of his left leg in the Battle of the Bulge. If he learned anything from the war, it was a simple trade — photography. On August 6, 1945, back in San Francisco from the European Theater, he listened in horror to accounts of the atomic bombing of Hiroshima, then Nagaski. Over the next few weeks he learned what had become of the atomic bomb program at Los Alamos. Yes, it was at least better that the U.S. had found the way to make a bomb than that Hitler had. It would be years before he accepted the deterrent capability of nuclear warfare.

In his photography studio on New Montgomery Street in San Francisco, across from the Palace Hotel, Bill Rader hosted the mayors of San Francisco, the boards of directors of major corporations, and an occasional model from I. Magnin putting together a personal portfolio. One day a young woman walked out of his dressing room in a bright red swimming suit and asked if this would work for the Macy's ad, which ran every day opposite Herb Caen in the *San Francisco Chronicle*. Thereafter, red was his favorite color. She soon weaned him from freedom and solitude of bachelorhood. But she often wondered why he never wanted to talk about what he did in the war.

Over the clinking of ice in drinks or the chatter of football on television, he sometimes told the story of how the Germans were foiled in their attempt to get the atomic bomb. Few listened to his wild stories. And as the years passed, the stories seemed lost in myth. But the image of Edwin O'Hara remained in his mind, in red. Not the reds of roses, nor the faded reds of cooked crab shells, nor the burnished reds of a hundred suns of summer settling under the Golden Gate, but the blood of patriots, spilled generously on the decks of ships.

LaVergne, TN USA
14 March 2010
175862LV00001B/40/P